He ambled toward her, as lazy as a long, cool drink of something wicked.

He confounded Maggie. It was absolutely ridiculous for a practical, grounded, capable twenty-nine-year-old woman to feel bowled over by the look in a man's eyes. But there it was. Darn it, Andy was so darling she just wanted to sip him in.

His mouth kicked up a grin long before he reached her. Those eyes of his were darker than a midnight sky. He gave the length of her a once-over, from the floppy socks to her jeans and baggy sweater to her hair flying every which way. Maggie knew darn well there was nothing in her appearance to earn that sizzling spark.

And then Andy asked her the question she'd been dreading all day.

"Remembered anything yet that I need to arrest you for?"

Dear Reader,

Hectic life? Too much to do, too little time? Well, Silhouette Desire provides you with the perfect emotional getaway with this month's moving stories of men and women finding love and passion. So relax, pick up a Desire novel and let yourself escape, with six wonderful, involving, totally absorbing romances.

Ultratalented author Mary Lynn Baxter kicks off November with her sultry Western style in *Slow Talkin' Texan*, the story of a MAN OF THE MONTH whose strong desires collide with an independent lady—she's silk to his denim, lace to his leather... and doing all she can to resist this *irresistible* tycoon. A small-town lawman who rescues a "lost" beauty might just find his own Christmas bride in Jennifer Greene's heartwarming *Her Holiday Secret*. Ladies, watch closely as a *Thirty-Day Fiancé* is transformed into a forever husband in Leanne Banks's third book in THE RULEBREAKERS miniseries.

Don't dare miss the intensity of an innocent wife trying to seduce her honor-bound husband in *The Oldest Living Married Virgin*, the latest in Maureen Child's spectacular miniseries THE BACHELOR BATTALION. And when a gorgeous ex-marine shows up at his old flame's ranch to round up the "wife who got away," he discovers a daughter he never knew in *The Re-Enlisted Groom* by Amy J. Fetzer. *The Forbidden Bride-to-Be* may be off-limits...but isn't that what makes the beautiful heroine in Kathryn Taylor's scandal-filled novel all the more tempting?

This November, Silhouette Desire is the place to live, love and lose yourself...to sensual romance. Enjoy!

Warm regards,

Joan Marlow Golan
Senior Editor, Silhouette Desire

Please address questions and book requests to:
Silhouette Reader Service
U.S.: 3010 Walden Ave., P.O. Box 1325, Buffalo, NY 14269
Canadian: P.O. Box 609, Fort Erie, Ont. L2A 5X3

HER HOLIDAY
SECRET
JENNIFER GREENE

SILHOUETTE *Desire*®
Published by Silhouette Books
America's Publisher of Contemporary Romance

T 114895

SILHOUETTE BOOKS

ISBN 0-373-76178-3

HER HOLIDAY SECRET

JENNIFER GREENE

lives near Lake Michigan with her husband and two children. Before writing full time, she worked as a teacher and a personnel manager. Michigan State University honored her as an "outstanding woman graduate" for her work with women on campus.

Ms. Greene has written more than fifty category romances, for which she has won numerous awards, including two RITAs from the Romance Writers of America in the Best Short Contemporary Books category and a Career Achievement award from *Romantic Times Magazine*.

One

White. When she opened her eyes, everything around her seemed bewilderingly white. White noise, white pain, white walls, white sheets.

The last thing she remembered was an explosion of vivid color. Vague pictures flashed in her mind from just before that. She was pretty sure she'd been driving. Alone. It had been snowing like a banshee, on a night blacker than a witch's soul. And then suddenly metal screeched on metal with the screaming sound of a crash, and all those jeweled colors had exploded in her head. Then nothing.

Really nothing. She swiftly realized she was lying in a hospital bed—and her body was creaking and groaning in too many places to worry that her brain wasn't functioning. She hadn't lost her mind. Just her memory. Her name, who she was, refused to come to her. There seemed nothing in her head but all that white fuzz…and a sick, terrible feeling that something bad had happened—something that she was responsible for.

"Well, now. You're finally waking up for us, huh?" The nurse who charged in had a round face framed by bustling, bouncing brown curls. The smile was sweet, but the eyes were all business. "Now don't try getting ambitious, honey, you just lie there. I'm going to take your pulse and get your blood pressure—"

Her throat was dry, her voice so thick that she had trouble getting the words out. "Something happened. An accident, I think—"

"Uh-huh."

"I was responsible? I caused it, didn't I? Oh God, was anyone hurt?"

"Well, I didn't hear much—no one ever tells us anything up here—but when Bertha wheeled you up from the ER, she said something about you being hit head-on. Didn't sound like your fault in any way to me." The nurse pried open her eyes, shot in a harsh spear of light, then flicked it off. "Feeling a little confused and disoriented, are we?"

"I can't seem to remember anything about it—"

"That's not at all unusual, hon. Just be patient and give yourself a little time. An accident's always a shock to the system, and after the body pumps up all that adrenaline, sometimes the mind just seems to shut down and take a little rest right after." The nurse squeezed two fingers on her pulse, then strapped a cuff on her upper arm. She seemed to have five hands, and when they weren't busy, she was talking.

"You don't need to worry about a thing. Not real likely you're going to win a beauty contest for a couple of days, but there were no broken bones, no internal injuries. I'll bet it feels like you tangled with the Marines, though, huh? You've got a prizewinning lump on your head and some Olympic-sized bruises, but you'll be perfectly fine and healed up before you know it. Doc Howard'll be in shortly. We've just been waiting for you to wake up. And the sheriff's waiting to see you, too—you know Andy Gautier? He's a sweetheart. If you feel up to it, he's got some questions about the accident—''

"I don't know what help I could be. I don't remember." Her voice was coming stronger, the whole hospital room sharpening in focus. The only thing still muzzy was her stupid mind. "Darn it. I *really* can't seem to remember. *Anything*—"

"Now just take it easy. If you're that worried about it, let's just try you out on some basics, okay? Do you know your name?"

To her relief, it came. "Maggie. Maggie Fletcher."

"There now. You aced that one. And your driver's license claims that you're twenty-nine, brown hair, green eyes, 110 pounds. That sound like you?"

Maggie would have nodded, except that any movement made her head feel like someone was crushing shards of glass in her skull. Wryly she admitted, "I think I lied about the weight."

The nurse chuckled. "Don't we all, dear. How about your address? You know that?"

"302 River Creek Road."

"Another ace. But we'll try a couple tougher ones. You know what day it is? Where you are?"

"Yeah. It's Friday—the Friday night after Thanksgiving. And I haven't been here before, but this has to be the hospital at White Branch." The concerned frown on the nurse's face was swiftly disappearing, and Maggie told herself she should be feeling equally reassured. It *was* all there. As if someone flicked the light switch on her memory, all the details of her life were relighting up. She could picture her cabin in her mind, knew what her job was, knew that she'd had Thanksgiving dinner at her sister's the day before. She hadn't lost...herself. Everything really was okay.

Except that she still couldn't remember a single detail after going to her sister's for the holiday dinner. The twenty-four hours before the accident were simply a blank. And that wouldn't particularly matter—except that she couldn't shake the anxious feeling that she'd done something seriously wrong.

The nurse obviously considered her ability to answer those questions as a sign there was nothing to worry about. "See now? What'd I tell you? You're starting to remember just fine. You just had a big jolt to your system, perfectly normal to feel fuzzy for a bit, and you've got a concussion to boot."

"But there's still this whole gap. I don't know where I was going, anything I did that whole day, why I was driving anywhere at night, the accident...you're not lying to me, are you? About someone else being hurt? About it being my fault?"

"If I knew more about the accident, I'd tell you. The truth is, I just don't. But—I'll make you a deal. You close your eyes and just rest for a few minutes. Now there's an IV in your arm—just glucose—but I don't want you getting out of bed without calling me. I'm just going to leave you alone and go get the doc. And if he okays it after seeing you, I'll let Andy in here for a couple minutes, and you can ask him more about the accident. Does that sound like a plan?"

The nurse left. Then Dr. Howard came and went. The two of them were a matched set. They both poked where it hurt, bossed her around, and went through identical litanies about "You're fine" and "nothing to worry about" and "a little temporary memory loss is common after a traumatic accident."

Once they both left, Maggie sank back against the pillow, exhausted from all this being taken care of. Outside the door, she heard the clattered wheels of a cart, phones ringing, voices echoing down the hall. Her only sojourn in a hospital before this was a few hours as an outpatient when she'd had her tonsils out at age six. She liked it even less now. The bed was too hard, the whole room so sterile and alien, and she'd never liked being fussed over.

She wanted to be home. Now, immediately. Her head burned like fire; her ribs ached; bruises were announcing themselves all over her body. If she were just home, in her own bed, everything would be better. She could rest. She could think. Maggie squeezed her eyes closed, disturbingly aware that that strange knife of guilt was still stabbing her conscience. There had to be a reason for it. She just had to make herself concentrate....

"Maggie Fletcher? Maggie?"

Her eyes shot open again. She'd forgotten about the sheriff. One look at the guy standing in the doorway, and Maggie doubted she'd make that mistake twice.

There were times she wouldn't mind meeting an attractive man. Tonight definitely wasn't one of them. She was feeling way too battered and beat up to conceivably have a functioning female hormone...but it seemed a couple stubborn ones perked up. The wayward thought skimmed through her mind that the stranger could probably arouse a woman from a coma without half trying.

"Maggie, I'm the sheriff, Andrew Gautier...Andy." He ambled toward the bed and stuck out his hand. The handshake barely lasted two seconds, no more than a polite greeting, carefully gentle. But his palm was warm and strong, his grip as straightforward as he seemed to be.

"I got a mixed review on whether it was okay to talk with you," he said wryly. "We can do this another time if you're not up for it. The consensus seemed to be if I'm real good and don't get y'all riled up, I can stay for a few minutes. There's always paperwork to fill out after an accident—not my favorite thing, but I was in the hospital, anyway, and I tend to procrastinate if I don't get it done. And Gert seemed to think you might feel reassured if I filled in some blanks for you on the accident as well."

"Yeah, that'd be fine. I'd appreciate it, in fact."

"Okay..."

He pulled up a chair, yanked a small spiral notebook from an inside pocket, and stretched out his long, lanky legs. He really was darling, Maggie mused. Not Mel Gibson, but he sure had the eyes.

He wasn't wearing any sheriff's uniform, dressed more like he'd been called from home and had to hustle out into the night. A beat-up leather jacket showcased linebacker shoulders, and both his charcoal sweatshirt and jeans looked like old, worn friends. His hair was cut short, starling-black, but it was thick and rumpled and still had a glisten from the damp snowy night. She thought he must have some Indian blood from the ruddy warmth of his skin tone and the sharp high cheekbones.

He was striking—so striking he could give any woman that nice, edgy *aware* feeling—but the eyes looked like trouble to her. Deep, dark, spicy. If he was the law, he sure wasn't looking her over in any lawful way. Those dark, exotic eyes prowled her face with more blunt masculine interest than she'd been treated to in quite a while.

Maggie mentally sighed. Obviously she was crazy, unhinged by the accident, imagining things. He surely

m too worried by her vast claims of previous run-ins
th the law. And she told herself there was no reason
t to skip the formalities and move to first names…his
b pinned him as a good guy, and his face was darn near
n atlas of integrity lines. Even without knowing him,
Maggie instinctively sensed he was hard-core honest. It
was just that other factor.

The man-woman thing. Any man who could arouse a
rapscallion set of female hormones in a battered woman
defined dangerous to Maggie. Interestingly dangerous.
Maybe darn-near fascinatingly dangerous—especially
since she hadn't felt that tug for a guy in a blue moon.
But she was all too aware that her judgment was temporarily and annoyingly goofy. To assume he meant something by that eye connection and those slow, lazy smiles
seemed foolish.

Cripes, she was just trying to sit up and a dozen aches
screamed distractingly at her, and her head pounded like
hammers at a carpenters' convention. Embarrassing her
no end, her hands were even shaky. "Well, what I started
to say…Andy…is that I bumped a fender when I was
sixteen, but that's the closest I've ever been to a real accident until tonight. This not being able to remember is
driving me crazy. I just want to go home. I'm positive
it'd all come back if I were just home, around my own
stuff…"

He seemed to sense where she was leading, because he
shook his head. "The way I heard it, Ms. Fletcher, there
sn't a chance in hell they're letting you out before to-
norrow morning."

"Yeah, I already tried arguing with them. But maybe
you'd consider using the power of the law on my side?"

"I'm real willing to use the power of the law. On their
le. Trust me, Gert'll watch over you better than a mom.

wasn't really communicating interest, and she had serious
stuff on her mind—nothing related to hormones. Yet the
first thing that blurted out of her mouth was an inane
"Cripes, I have to look like something a cat dragged
home from an alley."

He didn't miss a beat, but she caught just the edge of
a sneaky grin. "Yeah, I see some bumps and bruises, but
let's put it this way. If *my* cat'd dragged you home, he'd
be in tuna for the rest of his life." He patted his inside
pocket. "Hell. I've lost my pen again. I swear, if I buy a
dozen, I lose twenty-four." He vaulted out of the chair,
wagged a long finger in front of her nose. "Just stay here,
okay? No leaping tall buildings in a single bound until I
get back. I'll just go steal another pen from Gert—she's
used to it."

He was only gone a minute, came back, and stretched
out again with his notebook. "Okay, first thing I need to
ask you is who you want me to contact? We got your
basic stats and medical insurance information from your
wallet, but there was nothing in there about next of kin,
and I didn't find any other Fletchers in the phone book…"

"I have a sister living here. Joanna Marks. We don't
have the same last name because she was married—wid-
owed now." Even mentioning her sister's name brought
shadowed, troubling memories tumbling into her mind.
"But I don't want you to contact her. I'll call her. She'd
just panic if a policeman called, and I'm fine—"

"So the doc said—and that he wasn't letting you out
until tomorrow, earliest—but you're going to need someone to drive you home then. And some clothes. And I
think she'd probably want to know something like this
had happened to you—?"

"She would, but I just don't want to upset her." Her
sister was fragile right now, but trying to explain Joanna's

circumstances was none of the stranger's business and just took too much energy to even try. Maggie left it.

"Well, maybe there's someone else? Husband, boy-friend—?" There was just a spark of the devil in his eyes again, making Maggie feel like the question implied more than a fill-in-the-blank on his police form.

"No. Friends, of course...but it's the middle of the night. I can't see waking someone up and scaring them for no reason. And I'll call my sister in the morning." She swallowed hard. "As far as the accident, I keep trying to remember what happened, but it just won't come. I have this terrible feeling that I was to blame. The nurse—Gert—didn't think so, but I don't know if she was telling me the truth. Oh, God. Please tell me there wasn't a child involved—"

"Hey, take it easy there." Andy leaned forward, his notebook form forgotten. "A drunk driver swerved in your lane. Hit you head-on. There was no way you could have avoided him."

"You're sure?"

"I didn't actually see it, didn't get there until about ten minutes after it happened. But it was right on Main Street, and four witnesses saw the accident. They all gave me the same story, and the skid marks, condition of the cars—all the evidence—pointed in the same direction. In fact, my coming in here at all was just policy, to complete the report. But there was no doubt about how the accident occurred. You were *not* responsible."

Maggie searched his face. People fibbed for so many reasons—some of them well-meaning, like the doc and nurse who could have shaded the truth to reassure her. Yet she saw the character lines etched on his brow, the way Andy met her gaze like an unflinching straight shooter. She just sensed a man who'd never soft-soap the

truth. And that was great. She believed him. [...] se[...] if she hadn't caused the accident, she felt even [...] w[...] fused why that anxious, guilty feeling was stil[...] n[...] her conscience. "The man who smashed into [...] j[...] drunk driver—is he all right?"

"He won't be, after I get finished slapping cha[...] him and he sees Judge Farley," Andy said dryly [...] as far as injuries—he's less beat-up than you are[...] you haven't asked, but there's no way to pretty u[...] news about your car. I'm afraid it's totalled. Not t[...] have a mechanic's judgment, but the front end [...] crushed like an accordion—when I first saw it, I [...] afraid we weren't getting you out in one piece."

"I don't care about the stupid car." She backpedall[...] swiftly. "Well, of course I care. I'd rather eat clams than go car shopping, and I'm allergic to clams. But the car's insured. And it just doesn't matter, not compared to some-body being seriously injured. Just tell me one more time, okay? That no one else was hurt?"

"You were not responsible. And no one else was hurt." When she still studied his face suspiciously, he scratche[...] his chin. "Still having a hard time believing it, hu[...] Didn't anyone ever tell you it was okay to trust the law[...]

Well, he made her smile. "You think I should tru[...] guy I don't know from Adam?"

"Hell, no. Just me. Honest to Pete, I'm trustwort[...] a Boy Scout."

"Uh-huh. Well, the truth is, sheriff..." Maggi[...] tated. "Did I hear that 'sheriff' right? Or was it su[...] to be lieutenant or deputy? Not that I haven't h[...] and tons of run-ins with the law, but I'm not s[...] I'm supposed to call you—"

"Andy will do fine."

She saw the dance of humor in his eyes—

I'm telling you, she's ruthless. I've run across her be-fore—with my job, you get some bumps and bruises now and then. She'll drive you stark crazy with all the fuss-ing.''

"But that's exactly the problem. I *hate* people fussing over me.''

His mouth kicked in another grin. "Yeah, you kind of gave me that impression. Feeling helpless not exactly your favorite thing?''

"I can take care of myself.''

"I'll bet you can. But not tonight. I'm pretty sure you won't die from being spoiled for one night, will you?''

"Yes.''

Another grin—which definitely wasn't every man's re-sponse when Maggie got touchy on the subject of self-reliance. "I can't figure out how come I haven't met you before. In a small town like White Branch, I usually run into everyone sooner or later.''

"Well, I moved here about four years ago, but I don't usually run around robbing banks or causing trouble—except in my free time, of course. And car accidents just haven't been my thing. Until tonight, anyway. Darn it.'' She lifted her hand to the incessantly throbbing bump on her head. "This not being able to remember is just so stupid. I'm not the type to get shook up in a crisis. The opposite is true. I do rescue work, for Pete's sake. But the last twenty-four hours are just a total blank in my mind, and I can't seem to make a single detail come back.''

"Maybe it'll all come to you after a good night's sleep.''

"Maybe it'd come to me if I were just *home*.''

The curly-haired nurse popped her head in the doorway. "Andy! You low-down skunk. I told you ten minutes, max, and you're still in here!''

"I'm leaving, I'm leaving." Andy grabbed his note-book and battered Stetson from the bedside table and lurched to his feet. He winked at Maggie before turning around. "Gert—just so you know, she was trying to talk me into springing her out of here."

Maggie's jaw dropped at his betrayal—for all the good it did. Gert turned on her faster than a ruffled hen. "Over my dead body. You don't belong anywhere but right here, honey. A concussion is nothing to fool around with…" The nurse continued nonstop with impressive plans in-volving bedpans and ice chips and needles.

Maggie met Andy's eyes from around Gert's side and mouthed, "If we ever meet again, you're dead meat."

Andy murmured unrepentantly, "You go, Gert." But he hesitated right when he reached the doorway. There was just a two-second window when Gert had to take a breath before expanding on her health lecture. Two sec-onds. Then his eyes prowled her face one last time, and he said, "You can take it to the bank, Maggie. We'll meet again."

TWO

When Andy pulled in Maggie's drive two days later, he told himself the visit was justified. White Branch had little serious crime, but like any other community, there were always problems and always the potential for more. Part of the reason Andy loved his job was the power—not the power of his badge and gun, but the power to head off trouble before it started. If he had to flash a badge, he always figured he'd failed. Keeping a mean, keen eye on brewing trouble was an effective way of preventing disasters from escalating. For that reason, he regularly cruised certain neighborhoods. When anyone had an accident or traumatic problem, Andy just traditionally followed up to make sure things were okay.

Maggie had been in one hell of an accident.

Ergo, it was perfectly reasonable for him to accidentally be driving down River Creek Road and to stop by to see how she was.

Maybe the memory of those velvet-green eyes had hung
out in his sleep for the last couple nights. Maybe she was
the first woman since his four-year-old divorce who'd
itched on his mind like a mosquito. Maybe that spirit and
gutsy humor of hers had gotten to him—especially since
she'd looked so vulnerably battered in that hospital bed.
And yeah, maybe a peek at the alluring, shadowed swell
of one breast in the dip of her hospital gown had mangled
with his mind some, too.

But that had nothing to do with it.

Checking on people was simply his job.

As he pushed the gearshift to park, though, Andy
thoughtfully scratched his chin. Maggie was there. Standing by her front door. And she'd spotted his truck driving
in and turned her head to face him, so it was a little late
to slither back out of her driveway and hide himself in
the nearest avalanche.

It would definitely seem, however, that she was having
absolutely no difficulty recovering from her injuries...
judging from the enthusiastic way she had her arms
around another man.

She dropped her arms from the guy, and with a look
that was half curious, half puckish, promptly took a step
toward Andy's truck. As she was obviously coming to
greet him, he didn't figure he could pull a disappearing
act for at least a couple minutes. He swiftly pushed open
the door and climbed out.

A bitter wind instantly burned his cheeks and crawled
down his collar. Judging from the thick, murky clouds
roiling in from the west, he guessed they'd have a fresh
foot of snow by morning. Shame he hadn't taken those
ominous clouds as an omen—or else picked up a pre-
monition from those dancing green eyes of hers. Andy
was inclined to give himself a whack upside the head. No

thirty-four-year-old man—with a brain—should need any such omens to guess Maggie wasn't likely to be lacking male company.

"Well, hi again, Sheriff. This visit's a surprise. Did you think of something to arrest me for after all?"

He'd love to level a charge on her—notably disturbing the peace. His peace. But that wasn't something he was willing to confess. "I didn't figure I had to worry about you robbing any banks for a couple of days…you had enough bruises to keep you out of trouble at least that long. But I started thinking how remote your place is here and just thought I'd stop by. With your car out of commission, I wasn't sure if you had any wheels yet or might have needed some help."

"That was really nice of you. And I've certainly been trying to cause more trouble, but my nephew's been coming over every day by snowmobile to pitch in, bringing groceries and shoveling snow and everything else. Colin, come meet Sheriff Gautier. And Andy, this is Colin Marks, my sister Joanna's boy…."

Her smile had a lot of mischief in it, enough to make a man feel as though he'd been struck by lightning if he wasn't careful. Andy was still trying to recover from that smile when her words sank in. Nephew. Boy. And then the kid edged in front of her with a mannerly hand stuck out.

The boy was six-two—Andy's own height—with a cowlick sticking from his crown that probably added another inch, and the tea-brown hair and green eyes that easily labeled him as Maggie's kin. It was just the height and shoulder breadth that had Andy first assuming he was a grown man. A second look would have noted the gangling limbs and kid's awkward nerves, but Andy really hadn't been noticing much but Maggie. "Nice to meet you, Colin."

The kid shied back from the handshake, almost tripped over his own feet. "Nice to meet you, too." Those eyes skittered away from him fast. "Maggie, I got to be going. Mom'll be wondering where I am."

Andy had a cop's sixth sense that something was a little off, something more happening than just a teenager's awkward nerves, but maybe that was a mistaken first impression. The boy was obviously in a hustle to be gone. Maggie gave him another warm hug, and seconds later Colin was pelting for the snowmobile parked beyond her door. The machine engine roared on and the boy disappeared in a wake of snow.

"Fifteen?" Andy guessed his age.

"On the button. And I've got one other nephew, Rog. He's a year younger. Colin's more the high energy devil. He can get a wild hair now and then—but he's got a good heart. They both do. Their dad died last year, really threw both kids and my sis for a long painful loop. And before I tell you any more family history you don't want to hear—are you gonna keep an invalid outside freezing like this, or come in and have some coffee?"

"You don't look like much of an invalid." She looked breathtaking, in his objective opinion, but that wasn't to say Andy was buying her instant recovery quite at the wholesale price she was selling it. Her hair was worn loose and smooth to her shoulders, the silky brown color shot with honey and sunshine. She'd brushed it over her right temple, but he could still see the blotchy jewel colors of a bruise hiding beneath. A little careful makeup was obviously intended to conceal the circles under her eyes, and her red jacket collar was pulled up over a bandage on her neck. Maggie clearly didn't want anyone worrying about her—and that smile and full-of-hell spirit could easily distract a man from believing she'd ever been hurt.

"Well, all my best bruises are out of sight. They're so brilliantly colorful at this point that I'd love to show 'em off...but I'm afraid I won't do a strip search without a warrant, even for you, Sheriff." She hesitated. "Of course if you brought a warrant...?"

"Damn. No. But if you give me a second, I'll try to think up some charges—"

She chuckled. "Well, in the meantime, you like your coffee black or prettied up?"

"Black'd be great—but I don't want you going to any trouble."

"Nonsense, I'm freezing and could use something hot to drink myself. Come on in—and no, you don't have to take off your boots. This floor's seen snow before."

He stomped in behind her, shrugging off his jacket and placing it on a hook, next to where she hung hers. Under the outer gear, she was wearing a red turtleneck sweater over jeans and thick socks. Practical, comfortable clothes, but the loose cut of her jeans still showed off the curve of her fanny, and the sweater faithfully outlined ripe, firm breasts.

He was only watching her—he told himself—to judge if she were really as recovered from the car accident as she made out. Her movements seemed a little careful and deliberate to him, and he noticed she unconsciously pressed a palm to her ribs, as if the bruises there were still giving her trouble. Still, she was obviously getting around okay...which made it all too easy to shift his eyes to body parts that had nothing to do with any judicious, altruistic motives.

Forcefully he cut his attention to safer territory, while

she bustled around finding mugs and coffee. It wasn't hard to inhale her place in a single gulp.

The main floor was all open space, with the kitchen two steps up from the great room. The kitchen had brick walls, with an old-fashioned baking oven built into one. A vanilla-colored counter served as her table. Pots hung from a metal turnstile overhead, and spaghetti sauce simmered on the stove, the scent hot and spicy. Somehow he didn't think it came from opening a jar.

Below, the great room had one stone wall with a fireplace carved in—where a huge fire now roared, splashing sparks up the chimney. Two sets of double glass doors led to a wraparound cedar patio, with a view of secluded woods and a sharp ravine.

Maggie obviously liked blue. Furniture clustered in the room's center, blue couches, blue chairs, and a thick plush blue carpet made for bare feet. Nothing looked too pricey or overly color-coordinated...more like she just plain loved blue, and had chosen comfortable furniture big enough to curl up in.

She came up behind him, carrying two steaming mugs. "You might as well just tell me that you think the place is splendiferous. You'll hurt my feelings if you don't."

"I think it's beyond splendiferous. The whole place has a great hideaway feeling."

"Good boy." She grinned. "Built it myself. Or that's the story I tell. The truth is more like I couldn't possibly have handled the chimney or window fittings or plumbing. But I designed it, did the stonework and even the roof, so I figure I should get the lion's share of the credit."

"You won't get any argument out of me. I'm impressed. Seriously."

"Well, I almost killed myself tackling the roof...got my feminist knickers in a twist trying to play Super-

woman, when I should have had the brains to call for help.
But that's water over the dam.'' She took a fast sip from
a royal blue mug, and then motioned with it. "Come on,
I'll show you the rest. There isn't much. Just a sleeping
loft upstairs and my office and a storage room..."

The storage room combined laundry with a squared-off
space for sports gear—she was an experienced skier and
climber both, judging from the sturdiness of her equip-
ment—and she had a shop section with tools serious
enough to make a man drool. Her office, by contrast, was
pure female. A fancy high-tech computer setup was back-
dropped by girl stuff everywhere—scented candles and
bowls of potpourri, a hanging lamp with a fringy shade,
doodads and plants and pictures all fighting for the same
space.

"I take it you work from your home here?" he asked.

"Yeah. I do technical writing for Mytron, Inc.—they're
out of Boulder. I put together brochures and manuals for
them, that sort of thing. Once every few weeks—at least
once a month—I drive to Boulder and stay overnight, do
the face-to-face meetings kind of thing. Otherwise all I
really need are the phone, fax and modem to make the
telecommuting style work just fine. And I'll show you the
loft, but only if you promise to blind your eyes."

He had to chuckle. "Trust me, I've seen messy before."

"Uh-huh. I've heard big claims like that before. But
I'm talking *bad* messy. I'm talking disgrace. I'm talking
my sister is ashamed to know me, it's so bad."

An open staircase led up, where a waist-high balcony
viewed the stone fireplace below. The room *was* a clut-
tered mess, so much so that Andy's first thought was
Good, not too likely she'd had men sleeping over recently.
She whipped a bra out of sight, kicked a scrap of some-

thing pink under the bed, kept him chuckling, but a second and more serious thought had already followed the first…for all her apparent pep and lively spirit, she'd had some rough nights since the accident. Her queen-size bed had a white down comforter over salmon sheets. The sheets weren't just rumpled but untucked and pulled out, as if her dreams had been wild and troubled.

It was her architecture and design she was showing off, though, so he played along. The slanted roof had a skylight. The floor was carpeted with an Oriental rug that looked ankle-deep, but it was tricky to tell the pattern with the clothes and papers and books she had piled all over. The adjoining bathroom was big enough to have a square tub and a sit-down counter space. Her scent pervaded the bath. Soft, not sweet, not a scent he knew or could pin down, but distinctive and evocative. Like her.

"So how long have you lived here?" he asked.

"Almost four years now. Grew up in Colorado Springs, got the job at Mytron in Boulder when I graduated from school. But I really like country life, and my sister lived here, and when her husband was diagnosed with cancer about then…well. She's my family and they needed some help. It took a while to convince Mytron that I could do the job via telecommuting, but once I could see that was going to work out, I started looking at land to build a place. I really love the area."

"I was born and raised here, but I love it, too. Think I'm addicted to the mountains, and I can't imagine living in a place where buildings close you in." As they climbed back down the loft stairs, Andy again noticed the slight limp in her right leg. But a shadow moving on her porch snapped his cop's eyes in that direction…at least for a second. "Um, I believe you've got a deer on your patio."

"Yeah. Horace. He's a voyeur—around this time of

day, he usually shows up for a handout and peeks in my windows at the same time. He was in love last fall. God, there is no worse doofus than a buck in love. Brought Martha up to the patio to meet me. But I haven't seen her since, think the love affair must have gone sour, and he's gone back to peeking in my windows again."

Andy scratched his chin. "I'm not sure there's a charge for a sexually deviant deer."

"It's okay. I don't think Horace is highly motivated to reform anyway. The only neighbor who gives me real fits is Cleopatra—she's a raccoon, and I swear she steals anything that isn't nailed down or padlocked. You want a refill on that coffee?"

"Thanks, but I really should be going." Andy figured he'd stayed long enough for an uninvited visitor. "Never heard a name like Cleopatra for a raccoon before."

"Well, it seemed to fit. Honestly, if you saw her, you'd fall for her. All the guys do. She turns up pregnant every spring. I think it's in the eyes. She's got that fatal allure kind of thing."

"Maggie?" She made him chuckle again, imagining a raccoon with fatal allure. But they were ambling through the kitchen toward his coat. Andy considered he only had a few minutes left to get in anything serious, and Maggie cocked her head curiously when she heard the change in his tone.

"You're pretty isolated on this stretch of road. You really getting around okay since the accident?"

"Yeah. Really. Just fine."

"How about wheels?"

"Well, I have to get around to car shopping. A fate worse than death, if you ask me...but I'm fine for now anyway. Colin brought in some fresh groceries, and this time of year I've always got a stocked freezer because there's always at least one blizzard before Christmas. My sis has a car I could borrow if I had to. Really, I'm fine."

"You want some company car shopping?"

She'd paused to stir her spaghetti pot, glanced up. "Frankly, I wouldn't ask that of my worst enemy, Andy…but if you mean it…sure."

"Yeah, I mean it. The doc clear you to be out and around?"

"The doc ordered me to sack on the couch for a couple of days. I've rested until I'm blue in the face," she said dryly.

"So rested that the memory came back that was bothering you so much? You remember the accident now?"

It was the first time he saw that upbeat smile of hers falter. The shadows darkening her eyes made him think of that rumpled, torn-up bed. "No," she admitted quietly. "It's like that whole twenty-four hours before the accident was just wiped off my map."

He unhitched his leather jacket from the hook, burrowed into it, but his eyes stayed honed on her face. "It still just happened a few days ago."

"I know. And the doc must have told me a dozen times that it's really common. It's just…Andy, you don't know me. But I'm just not a person who folds in a crisis. I do rescue work. I hiked the Appalachian Trail alone when I was a kid. I'm no wimp. And especially since the accident wasn't my fault, I just don't understand why I can't make those memories come back unless something else serious happened."

She was so frustrated, she didn't seem to realize she was waving her spaghetti spoon around, spattering bits of red on her brick-tiled floor. Andy'd told himself—several times now—that it was time he left. But he instinctively stepped back into the kitchen to remove the lethal weapon from her hand. "I don't know what you're worried that 'something else' could be. You think you held up the local liquor store earlier that day?"

She had to know he was teasing, but he still couldn't win that smile back. "Heck. Maybe I did."

"And maybe cows fly. You're right that I don't know you, Maggie. Not well. Not yet, anyway. But offhand, I'd say the community's safe from your thieving, murderous ways. No offense. But I'd bet the bank you don't even hit the aspiring criminal ranks near any of the seven deadly sins."

"Hey, I speed," she said defensively.

"Well, hell. Let's cuff you right now and send you up the river."

"Darn it, Andy. Cut it out. You're making me feel better."

"Um…that was kind of the idea. In fact, seems to me if speeding's enough to give you a guilt attack—whether you can remember the specifics or not—I think you can safely rest your mind that you didn't rob any banks that day."

"Okay, okay, I admit I really doubt I did anything like that either," she said wryly, but then she sighed. "Only I keep waking up from these dreams. Nothing there. No substance. But my heart's pounding and my hands are sweaty. And the whole feeling just tastes like guilt, like I must have done something really wrong."

Andy was standing close enough to touch her, but he never intended to. His hand just somehow lifted to her cheek. The thing was, she seemed so troubled about that little twenty-four-hour memory lapse, when everything about her came across as strong and honest. She was a woman who damn near reeked integrity. He just wanted to communicate empathy, reassurance, and words alone didn't seem to be getting the job done. Possibly, conceivably, there were a few other small factors motivating his need to touch her, too.

Like the little swish in her behind when she walked. And the mischief in her humor. And her naming a deer Horace. And that elusive, evocative scent she wore. And the way being near her had his rusty hormones kicking up an unsettling tizzy, when that hadn't happened to Andy in a dog's age. He didn't lack for female company and he wasn't particularly wary—hell, every matchmaker in town had been throwing single women at him since the divorce. But leaping for an impulse just wasn't his way. He was too old to be impressed by a cute tush, and the kind of attraction that mattered took both time and seriously testing the compatibility waters before risking a bunch of grief that wasn't worth it.

So it was way too soon to even think about touching her.

And way out of line to be thinking about kissing her.

But once his palm touched her cheek, she lifted her face. Something was there. An expression that made him feel heart-punched, a connection in her luminous eyes that made his thumb instinctively stroke the edge of her jaw. She didn't move. She met his eyes, with all the wariness of a doe edgy with a buck in her territory. But she watched him on that long, long trip when he was bending down. And her lips were parted by the time he'd traveled the distance to hers.

Soft. She tasted soft and warm and tremulous. Both times he'd met her, she'd come across with that I'm-sturdy, I-can-take-care-of-myself routine. He believed it. It was probably why he'd taken to her so damned impossibly fast. But that wasn't how she kissed.

It'd been so long since he kissed anyone he figured he'd

forgotten how. Real quickly he realized that past experience wasn't going to rescue him from this problem anyway. This wasn't like any other kiss. She wasn't like any other woman.

His lips touched down, traced hers, in a testing questing kiss that she seemed to answer in the same language. It was like discovering a field of wildflowers in a snowstorm. Magic where it couldn't be. A time-out from reality that made no particular sense. He could smell her spaghetti sauce bubbling. Feel her kitchen lights glaring. His life was going fine, he wasn't all that lonely. Until he kissed her.

Her hand lifted, clutched at the folds of his leather jacket. Not pushing him away, just holding on. And that wooing, whisper-soft kiss kept coming on, like a spell being woven from her textures, her scents, the way her mouth fit his like she belonged to him, like he'd been missing her all this time and hadn't known.

He didn't try deepening the kiss. Didn't want to. But he kept thinking there had to be a catch. He kept waiting for the goofy, crazy feeling of a soul connection to disappear, for some common sense to give him a whack upside the head. Only it didn't. And she responded with the same wary, winsome, tremulous honesty, as if her sanity had been ransomed by that hushed, soft kiss the same as his had.

He got around to lifting his head. Eventually. She got around to opening her eyes. Eventually. They stared at each other like such a couple of shell-shocked teenagers that he had to smile. Eventually.

"I didn't come here expecting that," he said.

"I never thought you did."

"I just came to make sure you were okay. That's the truth."

''I believe you, Andy.''

''Seems to me, chemistry that strong pops up out of nowhere—it's nothing you can trust, just asking for trouble.''

''I couldn't agree more.''

''Uh-huh.'' He zipped up his jacket, grinned at her. ''You can count on it. I'll be back.''

Three

Maggie whisked the dinner plates into the dishwasher and sponged down the counters, but her gaze kept darting to the kitchen window. Predictably by the first of December, the sun had long fallen even this early in the evening. After two days of howling winds and incessant snow, the drifts swirled and curled in mystical shapes that looked like glazed icing in the moonlight. But her driveway was cleared—and empty, except for her sister's car. Andy wasn't due for another hour, so there was no reason on earth for her to start looking for him this early.

She grabbed a dish towel to wipe her hands, half amused, half exasperated to realize how nervous she was. Men never made her nervous. Offhand, she couldn't think of much in life that had ever intimidated her...outside of the strange, unsettling nightmares prowling her sleep since the accident. But that problem had nothing to do with Andy.

She didn't normally volunteer a house tour to strangers—much less expose her disastrously messy sleeping loft to a man's eyes. At the time...well, she hadn't known he was going to kiss her. Didn't know that kiss was going to knock her for six. But something had been kindling and simmering the two times she'd been around him. And the mistakes Maggie had made with men in the past all had the same roots.

Most guys claimed to be comfortable around a strong woman, but they really weren't. Someone looking for a vulnerable, traditional sweetie just wasn't going to find it in her. She'd been self-reliant and independent too long. These days, if there was even the tiniest hint of potential kindling, Maggie just believed in being frankly blunt about who she was. What you see is what you get. No faking it. Being nice just got in the way—if a guy was going to be scared off by her independence or messiness or anything else, better to know it and move on before either of them had a pile of hurtful emotions invested.

But Andy hadn't been scared off. At least not by anything she'd shown him so far. And for Maggie, that was downright rattling. Men *always* had some sweet, macho protective thing to say about a woman alone living in such a remote location. They fretted about her safety.

Safety was a relative term, Maggie mused. Trussed and blindfolded, she could capably cope with a dead furnace in a blizzard or a wounded moose wandering in her backyard. Piece of cake. Danger never had been a common word in her vocabulary—until meeting Andy, anyway. It struck her ironic humor buttons that something in those dark, sexy eyes made her feel distinctly unsafe.

And that was new and rattling, too.

"Maggie, for Pete's sake, I told you I'd do the dishes.

I was only gone for a minute! I didn't mean to leave you with all the work.''

Maggie whirled around when her sister Joanna emerged from the bathroom. "No big deal. The two of us didn't use enough dishes to take me more than two shakes."

"But you made the dinner. And I really meant to help—"

"So you can help next time." Although that would never happen, Maggie suspected. Growing up, the sisters had bickered like cats and dogs over stuff like this. Joanna was infamous for making the virtuous offer, but somehow always managed to be out of sight when it came time to do the dishes or the chore. But that was then, and this was now. "I made a fresh pot of tea—raspberry mint. You want a cup?"

"Maybe a short one. But I don't want to rush you on time. When's the sheriff picking you up?"

"Not until seven. And I keep telling you, it's no big thing. Andy just offered to take me car shopping." Maggie set a sturdy mug in front of her sister, feeling her heart catch just looking at Joanna's face.

Any nerves about meeting Andy were backburnered. She was so worried about her sister that she could hardly think. Steve had died more than a year ago. God knew the two had been inseparably in love, but Maggie felt at an increasing loss for how to help Joanna move past her grief.

Her sister was five years older than she, and in Maggie's view, the real beauty in the family. Now, though, Joanna's long blond hair was lanky, her elegant features drawn, the huge almond-shaped green eyes deeply shadowed. Her slim white hands trembled even holding the mug of tea.

Maggie had always been the strong cookie of the pair.

From the time her brother-in-law was diagnosed with cancer, she'd naturally stepped in. Long before Steve died, she'd had her sister over for dinner once a week, took her nephews all the time, stopped by the house whenever she could. But Steve had been gone a year now, and Joanna seemed more fragile instead of less. Increasingly everything seemed to throw her sister, from finances to leaky faucets to snowstorms. Joanna paced the floor at night, worrying about her two sons. She didn't sleep right, didn't eat right, didn't take care of herself.

Maggie could fix the stupid leaky faucets and sneakily pad Joanna's bank account, but she didn't know how to fix her sister. The two may have fought ferociously growing up, but they'd also always been hopeless gigglers. Lately it was tougher than climbing a mountain to win a smile out of Joanna.

"Hey, did I tell you how great Colin's been to me? I don't know how many times he's been over since the accident. Shoveled my walk without asking, stacked my wood. What's wrong with him?" Maggie teased.

"He always worshiped the ground you walked on. And you're terrific with both boys. I can't seem to get either one of them to talk to me…" Joanna spilled a little tea. "I don't seem to be doing anything right lately."

Maggie hustled for a cloth to wipe up the spill. "Listen, you goose, you're doing fine. Quit being so hard on yourself. Do you remember either of us talking to Mom or Dad when we were teenagers? There's just this stage where it's hard to talk to a parent. But I do think you should get out more."

"Mags, I'm not ready to date anyone."

"So don't date. But you could take up skiing, or aerobics…you love cards, maybe you could find a euchre club. There's a dozen things you could do to get out, meet people again—"

"You've got ten times more courage than I do, Maggie. I'm just not good with charging into things the way you do. Speaking of which…do you know this guy you're going out with tonight?"

"Andy? Nope. But being the sheriff, I think it's a fairly safe bet he isn't a serial killer on the sly. And how well do you have to know someone to spend a couple hours car shopping with them?" Maggie asked wryly.

"I still don't know why you just didn't ask me. I'd have taken you. Or you could have borrowed my car. You do so much for me all the time, Mags, and you never let me return the favor—"

Cripes, they were going down another long, mournful road. "Come on, you," Maggie said humorously, "I couldn't see turning down guy help. Not on this. What the two of us know about mechanics would fit in a thimble with room to spare."

"Well, that's true. Clothes shopping'd be a lot more fun," Joanna admitted. "For that matter, Christmas is coming and I haven't even started that shopping yet."

"Good. Neither have I. How about if we block off next Thursday morning and get a start on it together?"

It took a while to get her sister on a more upbeat track. By the time she had Joanna bundled up and headed out the door, though, headlight beams were turning in her drive. Andy. And she hadn't had two seconds to brush her hair or yank on her good boots, much less slap on some lipstick.

Still, she stood freezing in the open doorway. Andy pulled up next to her sister's car and stepped out. The yard light didn't beam far enough for her to identify his vehicle, but it was something low and black instead of

the car with the sheriff's logo. He stopped long enough
to introduce himself to her sister and exchange a few
words.

Before driving off, Joanna turned around to level her a
look. Maggie knew That Look from their childhood. It
meant she'd neglected to tell her sister some critical tidbit
of information...such as that her casual don't-sweat-it
company for the evening was a priceless hunk, for example.

Which he was. He ambled toward the door, as lazy as
a long, cool drink of something wicked, his boots crunch-
ing in the snow, his jacket open over a thick black
sweater.

Her sister's car lights disappeared down the road, and
then there was nothing but him—and a wham-slam of
magic that confounded Maggie. It was absolutely ridiculous for a practical, grounded, capable twenty-nine-year-
old woman to feel bowled over by the look in a guy's
eyes. But there it was. She hadn't suddenly stopped worrying about Joanna; no problems in her job or life had
instantly disappeared. But darn it, he was so darling she
just wanted to sip him in.

His mouth kicked up a grin long before he reached her
back porch. Those eyes of his were darker than a midnight
sky. He gave the length of her a once-over, from the
floppy socks to her jeans and navy angora sweater to her
hair flying every which way. Maggie knew darn well there
was nothing in her appearance to earn that sizzling spark.

"Remembered anything yet that I need to arrest you
for?"

Sparks or no sparks, she had to laugh. "I haven't
robbed any banks since the accident—but that's all I'm
willing to swear to."

"Uh-huh. That memory loss was the story you gave me

last time. I was a little afraid you'd extend that amnesia business to tonight, knowing how thrilled you were at the idea of car shopping.''

"If I didn't have to have transportation, nothing could talk me into doing this," she admitted. "And I did think about cancelling. This is an awful thing to ask anyone to do, Andy.''

"As I remember it, I offered. You're not putting me through anything I didn't volunteer for. And, speaking for myself, I think this is like toothpaste.''

She'd just turned around to pull on her suede boots and grab her jacket and purse. "Toothpaste?''

"Yeah. There's just no point in getting all hot and heavy and involved with a woman, only to find out she squeezes the toothpaste tube from the top. I mean, where can you take a wild, immoral affair after that? You just know it's going downhill.''

"Um...I take your point. I think. But I'm not exactly sure how you got from toothpaste-tube-abusers to car shopping?''

"Car shopping with a woman," Andy informed her, "gets all those down-and-dirty details out of the way right up front. If you go for the awkward first date, out-to-dinner thing, what do you ever learn? Nobody's honest. Both sides are too busy tiptoeing around each other, trying to be ultra nice.''

"I sure agree with that. First dates, you're just kind of stuck, being on your shaved and perfumed behavior, so to speak," Maggie replied with a chuckle.

"Uh-huh. But if you do something like this, now..." Andy thoughtfully scratched his chin. "You find out what kind of car *really* seduces her. Like whether she's interested in looking under the hood or just goes for a showy exterior. Whether she wants to know all the safety features

ahead, or that's just not a concern. How much power turns
her on—or off. Whether she likes a slow, steady accel-
eration or a fast, rough ride.''

"Whew." Maggie zipped up her jacket and propped
her hands on her hips. "That lazy, country boy drawl is
really good, Gautier. For a minute there, I almost believed
you were talking about cars.''

"I was, I was.''

"Uh-huh. And cats fly. For the record, I don't look
under anybody's hood on a first date. On the other
hand…'' Maggie threaded on gloves as she hiked past
him. "I think you've got a valid theory going. I'd rather
do this than the out-to-dinner thing any time—for your
sake, really. If by some remote chance you can survive
car shopping with me, the future probably stretches in
front of us with limitless possibilities. At the very least,
you'll unquestionably earn hero status, sainthood, a couple medals for courage…''

"A drink when this is over?"

"That, too.''

"Well, hell. Let's go find you a chariot, ma'am, and
get that little chore over with.''

By the time they were belted in his dark car and wing-
ing down the road, Andy had conquered the urge to kiss
her. Actually, the marvel wasn't that he'd behaved himself. Hell, he always behaved himself—unless invited otherwise. But he wasn't expecting the power of that temp-
tation. A divorce gave any man an instant Ph.D. in
caution.

And he *felt* cautious with Maggie. The problem with
fireworks was that they fizzled out so fast. A light show.
Then phfft. So he'd logically figured out that magical red-
hot sexual pull would settle down if he just saw her, spent

some time with her again. Sizzle mattered. Sizzle was nice—deliriously nice, in her case. But Andy was wary of letting his hormones get in a dither before finding out if they had the kind of charge between them that counted.

That was the theory. A double-dose dither had turned out to be the reality. One look at those fading, vulnerable bruises and his first instinct was to pull her into his arms. One look at that soft red mouth connected directly to a hot wire in his groin. The way she cocked her chin, the swish of silken hair framing her face, the gutsy pride in the way she stood, the sparkle and devil in her eyes…hell, there was no one detail that heated his hormones to a bubbling simmer. It was just her. The whole package. No woman had tangled his nerves up like this in a long, long time. He couldn't stop wondering if she'd take all that sparkle and devil and honesty with her under the sheets. Under his sheets.

Cars, he thought.

He needed to keep his mind on cars.

"A lot of people out tonight," Maggie remarked.

"Yeah. The early Christmas shopping crowd, I'm guessing." His windshield wipers fretfully scraped a haphazard splash of snow. Main Street was well lit, but he could see pedestrians slip-and-sliding. The roads were icy slick and the temperature was pushing a mean subzero. Andy doubted most people would normally choose this season or time of day to car shop, but most people didn't see any accidents the way a cop did. Personally he thought it was an ideal time to test the mettle of any vehicle. "So…are you ready to get down to brass tacks? We've got three car dealerships in Silver Township. Probably help if you'd give me a clue what you're looking for."

"Something that starts in winter and doesn't give me any trouble."

"Okay. That only limits it to about five thousand models. Anything just a little more specific on your wish list?"

"Well…if it can't behave on snow and rough back roads, it's no good to me. And I need some room. Like space for skis in the winter, backpacks and tents in the summer. The car that was totalled in the accident? It was new. It was pretty. It had cream upholstery. It was the dumbest thing I could possibly have bought, for me."

"So you need more of a practical, utility vehicle. Sturdy, four-wheel drive, dual brakes…lots of good choices we can look at in that ballpark. Now to the dicier questions. I don't want to pry. But before we get near a car salesman, it'd help if you gave me a ceiling and a general idea what your price range is."

She chuckled. "Money isn't a problem, Andy. I can handle that part."

He heard the chuckle, but he also caught the teensy stiffening in her shoulders. Oops, best not go down that road, he thought dryly.

But as they drove into the first car dealership, he felt increasingly relaxed. He was pretty sure how this was going to go. Not that he knew Maggie so well, but certain things just seemed obvious. She had a couple tons of pride and a big thing about independence. Ergo, it was tough for her to admit to a weakness, and if she'd been bamboozled on price or mechanics or a bad car choice before, it was just natural that she'd be a little prickly.

Like any lawman in a small town, Andy knew the business owners on a first-name basis. He was with her, so she wasn't gonna get bamboozled this time. He just had to be careful to help her out in an unobtrusive, tactful way. And the second ingredient Andy figured he needed to make this venture go smoothly was a couple buckets of patience.

Maggie was, after all, female. And even a bad marriage could teach a guy certain things. Shopping with women for anything was like trying to communicate with an alien species. They needed time. They needed to compare. They needed space to be indecisive. They took forty years to make up their minds on anything.

Blazing white neon lights illuminated a half acre of cars. Andy stepped out and plastered on his soul-of-patience smile. No guy she'd ever been with—and for damn sure no guy she'd ever kissed—was ever gonna be as patient as he was.

Cut and dried.

Harvey Lyman barrelled out of the building the instant he saw them climbing out of Andy's car. "Hi there, folks!" Harvey had a fluff of white hair, cheeks like apples and a gut like a watermelon—four weeks from now he'd be playing Santa, and God knew he had a face that could inspire trust in the unsuspecting. His smile sagged a good half inch when he recognized Andy.

"Good to see you, Sheriff Gautier." They pumped hands, did the obligatory how's your dad, isn't this snow something small talk routine. "So what can I do for you? You're looking at cars?"

"I brought a friend. She's looking. *Just* looking tonight, but...." Andy half turned to introduce Maggie, and found her gone. No tea-brown bobbing head anywhere, no puffy down-filled green jacket that matched her eyes, no nothing.

Harvey was chugging steam by the time they caught up with her. Maggie had just finished circling a sporty white utility vehicle with a dark gray interior. She lifted her face in a smile when she saw Andy. "This'll do," she announced.

"Yeah, I think that's one of the good choices that'd work for you, but..." But he assumed she was kidding.

She wasn't kidding.

There were dozens of other cars to check out, and they hadn't even strolled through the other dealerships. She hadn't sat behind the wheel. He strongly suspected she hadn't even glanced at the sticker price.

Harvey could smell a sucker at fifty paces, but even he had to choke out a suggestion that she must want to look around. No dice. Maggie patted the big car's rump. "Really, this fits the bill. Right size. Colors I can live with. I don't see any reason not to just get this over with—"

Harvey was in danger of an imminent heart attack. He'd probably never smelled such an easy sales commission in his entire thirty years in the business. Still, he managed to puff out, "You're making a brilliant choice, a fine vehicle, dependable—"

"Shut up, Harvey. Maggie, you're not buying a car you haven't even sat in." Harvey produced the keys faster than a finger snap. She climbed in, sat down, climbed back out again.

"Okay. Feels good. Now can we just get this over with? Where do I pay?"

Harvey went into a spasm of coughing. Andy clamped a firm hand on his shoulder. "She's going to test drive it. And then she's going to think about it. Long and hard. The only reason she's smiling is because that sticker price is so funny. You hear me, Harv?"

Harvey not only wasn't listening; Harvey had completely forgotten who'd saved his nephew from a drunk-and-disorderly charge at Babe's bar last year. He only had eyes for Maggie, and they were big and soulful and sincere. "You just take it for as long a drive as you want to, honey. Enjoy yourself. It's such a classy car, I can't even think of another vehicle that'd be more perfect for you—"

Once Harv was shut out and they were both seated inside the car, Maggie said, "Look, I can see you're getting exasperated with me—"

On a witch-black night in a pitch-black car, he could still see the wariness in her eyes. Wariness that hadn't been there before. "Are you kidding? I'm not remotely exasperated."

Exasperated, no. Dumbfounded, yes. Naturally he kept quiet while she fiddled around, learning where the gauges and controls were, and finally putting the baby in gear. Most people test-drove vehicles in daylight and perfect conditions, but Andy had cleaned up after too many car crashes. Her seeing how the vehicle handled on snow-crusted roads at night was a prizewinning idea, in his view. Only she'd had enough after one round-the-block.

He made her drive it on the highway for a good ten miles, then cajoled her into handling it in an empty ice-slick parking lot. But that was all he could talk her into. Actually, he thought the vehicle was a good choice for her and Harvey was likely to make the best deal—he'd never have brought her here otherwise. He just couldn't believe any woman could make up her mind faster than a speeding comet—much less stick to it.

Harvey was waiting outside when they drove back in, wearing a three-hundred-watt smile to help light the night. "You loved it, didn't you? I just knew you would. And I'll help you all through the financing, little lady, don't you worry about a thing. You've picked a great car, a really great car—"

"Harvey," Maggie said gently, "we're not going to survive the next five minutes together if you call me 'little lady' or 'honey' again. Just call me Maggie, okay?"

Twenty degrees, tops, wind so mean it had to be twenty below with the wind chill, but Harvey's forehead abruptly beaded sweat. "Of course, Maggie—"

"And I won't need financing. I'll pay you in cash."

Harvey's jaw dropped. Hell, so did Andy's.

"Well, not cash," she swiftly corrected herself. "I meant a check. I don't actually have that kind of cash on me. But a check's okay, isn't it?" Her gaze darted from one man to the other. "I mean...I assume I can't drive it home, that you'll have to call the bank tomorrow to make sure it clears and all, but..."

"Um, Maggie..." Andy swept an arm around her shoulder to steer her out of Harvey's earshot. He wasn't sure what to say—not without bucking into her pride— and those shoulders of hers were stiff, that beautiful jaw of hers jutting at an awfully defensive angle. "Sweet pea, I'm getting the feeling that maybe you haven't bought too many cars before?"

"Well...no. The thing is, my parents died, Andy. Not together, but about the same time. My mom got sick, pneumonia they couldn't lick, and my dad was on the way to the hospital when someone smashed into him. We were pretty young—Joanna just out of college and I was in my first year—"

"Aw, hell. I'm sorry."

"I didn't tell you to make you feel bad. And I didn't mean to get into all that—I was just trying to explain about the cars. Joanna already had a car, so I ended up with my parents' vehicle, drove it for years. When it finally quit...well, the car that just got totalled is the only one I ever bought of my own. And that experience was just as awful and nerve-racking as this one."

Andy was suddenly getting a whole different picture of why car shopping upset her so much. There'd never been a dad or someone to teach her the basic strategy. "Well, to begin with…it's pretty rare people pay for cars in cash."

"Yeah. I know. The guy about had a fit the first time—like he changed his mind and didn't even want to sell it to me? Cripes, he gave me such a hard time I almost walked out. If I hadn't needed the wheels, I would have."

"I understand. But thing is, the sticker price isn't the whole story. If you want the car, you want the car. But it's real likely Harv'll go down some significant dollars if we give him a chance to sharpen his pencil. And the other thing is, you just might not want to deplete any interest-earning savings or capital to pour into a single giant expense like this."

"Well, I get you on all that. But I'm just no good with dickering, Andy. And I hate owing anybody anything. I make a good salary. I have the money. And if I were to get sick, there's just me to take care of myself, so the idea of debts hanging over my head gives me hives."

"Well, we don't want you in any situation that gives you hives," he said teasingly. But before this whole deal was over, Andy thought there was a pretty good chance he'd be suffering from hives himself.

Four

"You've more than earned a drink. I warned you that shopping for cars with me would be a trial, but I don't think you believed me. What are you up for? You a Scotch man? Whiskey? Brandy?" Maggie stepped in the back door, switched on lights, jettisoned her jacket and boots and aimed for the kitchen.

"Scotch, if you have it. But on the short side. And I enjoyed doing this with you, Maggie, it was no trial."

"Come on. I didn't actually see you tearing out your hair, but I'm guessing you were thinking about it. I *know* you thought I was nuts to pay for the car outright like that." She fumbled in the back of the cupboard for the dusty bottle of Scotch, then splashed some in a glass for him and poured a thimbleful for herself. She dropped in one ice cube, then a second. Possibly her movements were clumsy because her fingers weren't unfrozen yet, but she had a feeling it was Andy's proximity. He'd been affecting her that way the whole darn evening.

"I think you chose a vehicle that's gonna work for you fine. And no, I didn't agree with the way you bought it, but hell, that's another toothpaste thing. You ever met a couple who didn't fight over money?"

She carried both glasses down to the living area, then turned on more lamps. Lots of lamps. *All* the lamps. Just so Andy wouldn't get the idea that inviting him in this late meant she was setting up some cozy, romantic, dim-lit seduction scene. Just so *her* mind wouldn't travel down those wayward roads either. "Come to think of it—no."

"Same here. I think it must be an invisible relationship rule." Andy folded his jacket on a chair and settled on the couch. "Doesn't seem to matter whether the couple's married or single, ninety years old or eighteen, rich, poor, happy with each other or not. Men and women just seem to fight over money. So we were gonna argue about that sooner or later. We just got our feet wet a little quicker than most. And Maggie?"

"What?" The room was as glaring bright as daylight, no more lights to turn on. She curled up on the couch cushion across from him and gulped a sip of Scotch, hoping it would settle her hopscotching nerves. It wasn't like she'd never had a man over. Andy was just...different. He'd stretched out his legs and looked like a long, lazy, relaxed panther in that bulky black sweater and ink-black hair that matched his eyes. Every female instinct had seriously assessed and judged him a Good Guy through and through. It was just something about the way he looked at her that made Good Girl thoughts fly out of her head.

"I hate to break this to you, but fighting over money— with you—was an enlightening experience. I don't know if you still have that little twenty-four-hour amnesia problem that was bugging you around the time of the accident?'' At her startled nod, he continued. ''Well, I saw what kind of lying, larcenous con artist you were with the car dealer. I just really, really don't think you need to worry that you robbed any banks that day.''

''Hey, I could have.''

''Uh-huh. The moon could turn pink, too. But offhand, I'd steer away from poker games. I'm not sure you could bluff your way through a lie if a knife were at your throat.''

''All right, all right, I admit I don't fib very well. But there are still a total of seven deadly sins on that infamous list, aren't there? Don't start making wild assumptions that I'm a good person, Andy. I still could have done something that you have to arrest me for.''

Andy's eyes flashed over the rim of his Scotch. ''Somehow I don't see an arrest in your future, but hey, I've got a pair of handcuffs if you want to try 'em out. I can't say that's normally my fantasy, but I swear I'm willing to oblige anything that's on your mind—''

''Gautier! Behave yourself!'' She grabbed a newspaper and thwacked his knee with it, but that only made him chuckle. The scold wasn't likely to have much effect when she was laughing, too, but Maggie thought this just wouldn't do.

It wasn't the kinky vision of being handcuffed by Andy in a dark room with silky sheets that had her face flushing. Or only partly. He'd done it twice before—brought up her little memory loss and gone out of his way to lightly tease and say something to reassure her.

She still hadn't remembered those lost twenty-four hours. And every single night since the accident, she'd wakened up with her heart pounding and this crushing, anxious feeling of guilt. It was driving her nuts, that she couldn't remember. And though Andy couldn't know that, his teasing her really did make her feel reassured—which was pretty crazy, considering how little she knew him.

But there was a solution to that, she mused. Getting to know him.

"We're going to talk about your work," she said firmly.

"You think that's safer than talking about handcuffs and wicked fantasies?"

"Significantly," she said dryly. "I'm serious, though...I'd really like to know what your job's like...why and how you decided to wear a badge, what kind of things you handle in an average day?"

"Well...as far as how I got into it...my great-gramps was a Frenchman by the name of Raoul Gautier. Came west to fight the Indians, only that goal got all goofed up when he fell in love with a Cheyenne lady by the name of Running Deer. A lot of folks didn't accept their marriage too well, which ticked him off enough to change philosophies. He decided peace was a lot more worth fighting for than war, and that kind of became an enduring thread in the men of the family. My grandfather wore a badge, so did my dad."

She tucked a leg under her as he drawled out that mini-tale. She suspected his great-gram was behind those high cheekbones and liquid dark eyes, but the devil's dry humor seemed genetically, distinctly male. "So there's a lot of family tradition behind you. And that's a thought-provoking idea—going into law enforcement as a way to fight for peace."

"Doesn't make sense to everyone. My ex-wife sure couldn't see it for grass. I think she envisioned being married to a crime-fighter as a lot more exciting, hated everything about country life. I'm the reverse, like everything about it. In a place this small, you can be more flexible with the law than in an inner city. And you've got a real shot at making a difference, preventing trouble instead of chasing after problems after the fact, when it's too late to do much but clean up the mess through the court system.''

Maggie filed away the comment about his ex-wife, sensing he didn't want to pursue it. Other things he'd said more immediately intrigued her, besides. ''I'm not sure what you meant by 'more flexibility.' Isn't the law the law? Right is right?''

''Sure, right's always right,'' Andy agreed. ''But people's problems don't always fit in a nice little rule book.''

''Such as?''

''Well…'' He finished the last of his Scotch and set the glass down. ''Like Mary Lee and Ed Bailey get into a fight about every two months. She hits him around when she gets liquored up. Ed needs to figure out why he stays in an abusive relationship. Hell, what he needs is a women's support group, but damned if I can picture him going for that.''

She had to chuckle at his wry expression. ''You're making it sound funny, but somehow I'd guess that's a really serious, touchy thing to deal with.''

''Touchy comes with the job. Myrtle Tucker's another one. She's a hundred-and-three, and there's no way she should be living alone. But the last social worker who tried to put her in a rest home was met by Myrtle at the door with a shotgun. Wouldn't make a lot of sense to haul her up on charges, now would it? I set up a round-robin of neighbors to check on her, and I stop by a couple times a week myself.''

''Don't stop now. Tell me some more about the kinds of things you handle.''

Andy scratched his chin. "Well, there's Susan Harkins. Waitress at Babe's. I wouldn't be telling you her name, except she's never kept it a secret herself. When she runs a little short on her credit card bill, she's a little inclined to charge for, um, extra services after hours."

"Oh, God. Gossip. I love it. She really does the lady of the night thing?"

"Did, not does. At least I'm sure as hell hoping it's past tense. But she's another example of someone who technically pushed the law, only nobody gained anything by throwing her in jail. She started out with the self-esteem of a turnip, couldn't manage her money. Got a little help, things got better. And then sometimes people just get in a little twilight zone type of trouble..." Andy hesitated.

"Like what?" Maggie prompted him.

"Well, like this guy...best I keep this story anonymous. But his wife bought him, um, a sex toy for his birthday. Put the kids to bed, turn out the lights, everything's going fine...until their toy got stuck. There was no way in the universe the wife could get him to go to a hospital and risk the doc telling all his neighbors, so they called me."

"Andy! You're kidding!"

"Believe me, I wish." Andy rubbed the back of his neck. "It isn't all stories like that. What I'm trying to say is that we hardly have a hotbed of crime here, more like we just need a presence. Town our size, all we have is me and two part-time deputies—Mavis and John. Most of the time, that's enough. Thief rings coming in from out of town, drugs from the outside—state or feds come in to help us. But there're 250 kids in the school. They aren't all saints. People die, babies decide to get born in impossible places, deer get hit in the road, neighbors fight, kids get in trouble…things happen. Who're you gonna call but a cop?''

When Maggie stayed silent, Andy swung his legs off the coffee table and leaned forward. "I didn't mean to run on. Afraid I can get pretty wound up when I talk about my work.''

"You didn't run on. I could listen all night. But I admit, you're scaring me a little, Sheriff.''

"Scaring you?'' His eyebrows shot up in surprise.

"Yeah. I hate to confess this in public. Corny values aren't exactly in. But I've always had this problem, believing in the old traditional values like integrity. And honesty. And standing up to make a difference in the place where you live.''

His smile came slow and lazy. "Yeah? So where's the scary part?''

"Well, I can't just come out and tell you I admire you, Gautier, because it could go straight to your head. But I like the way you talk about your job. And I like the way you feel about it.''

Andy slowly stood up. "Uh-huh. Does that mean when you walk me to the door that you're not gonna punch me when I make a pass?''

"It means you'd better not push your luck, big guy, because you are going home.''

"Tonight,'' he qualified. As he reached down to pluck his jacket from the blue chair, his eyes met hers with an unspoken promise that another night could have an entirely different ending.

She could feel that look in his eyes clear to her toes. But memories of her recent nightmares suddenly shadowed her smile. "Maybe you should be glad I'm kicking you out. Who knows what kind of scarlet woman you could be getting involved with? You really don't know me, Andy."

He extended a hand, and clasped her fingers tight as they ambled toward her back door. "I survived the car shopping thing, didn't I? I was hoping that would give me brownie points worth six or seven dates in normal circumstances."

"It does," she assured him with mock gravity.

"And I wouldn't say you're a stranger. I picked up some dark secrets about you tonight. You couldn't exactly hide your cutthroat, thieving character when you were dealing with Harvey. And then I watched you, coming back home, turning on every light in the downstairs. I think you were worried I was going to pounce the minute I got in the door."

"I wasn't worried," she said swiftly.

"Yeah, you were."

There seemed no corner in the room where she could hide from those dark, magnetic eyes. "I'm suspicious of feelings that come on too fast, Andy. And I just don't hop in bed fast. Ever. You could have misunderstood, my inviting you in this late."

"Well, we can clear that air real fast. I don't hop in bed either. It's no fun. Getting naked's easy, getting intimate is a whole different thing. The whole climb it takes to get there is too damned much fun to rush. But I am telling you, Maggie, that I don't have a single honorable intention anywhere near you, so be warned."

She was warned. He made it as far as the kitchen doorway before he dropped his jacket, swung her to face him, and pounced. Pounced slowly. So slowly that she could see his entire expression change in the blazing glare of all the lights she'd turned on. So slowly that she saw his face tilt, his mouth aiming for hers, his dark eyes taking

her in so intensely that he made her shiver. She had ample
time to skitter away if she'd wanted to.

She'd never skittered from anything she was afraid of
before and didn't now. Still. His lips touched down on
hers like a warm, smooth, slow connection to lightning.
There was no way she could liken it to less. The damn
man. She'd been so positive that spending time with
him—especially an evening devoted to a horrible chore
like car shopping—would surely obliterate that magic
foolishness.

Only the problem seemed to have magnified instead of
diminished. His mouth had barely connected before a
smoking sizzle was hurtling through her bloodstream,
shooting awareness to her pulse and shimmering heat to
her nerves. He tasted like that golden Scotch, smooth, but
with the heat of a kick right behind it.

His hands slid down her ribs, around her spine, pulling
her into him. That first taste of her mouth seemed to inspire him to try another, in a mercilessly slow kiss that
involved tongues and teeth. The glaring lights should have
sabotaged any romantic feelings. But her eyes closed and
somehow there was just him and that crazy, goofy magic
feeling. Like she'd never been kissed before. Like he
wiped the memory of any man who'd ever been in her
life clear off the blackboard.

His mouth trailed a chain of kisses down her jaw and
throat. She tried to gulp in air. There wasn't any. Her
mind retracted all the nice things she'd thought about him.
She'd been dead wrong. He wasn't a good man. He was
trouble, clear through. He dipped down for another dark,
wet kiss that scrambled any sane thought in her head. His
big warm palms pushed at her sweater until they found
bare skin at her spine. She could feel his arousal, growing

hard and hot, until her fingers formed fists behind his neck, clutching, holding on.

He was going to pull her sweater off, she knew, and felt a shiver of anticipation...maybe of fear. This wasn't a kiss, an embrace, headed for a nice little goodbye at the door. It was an invitation to murder and mayhem. How could she have guessed a lawman could induce such amoral, lawless feelings? She never remembered feeling desire like this, hunger like a shock wave, wanting that seeped through her like a stolen secret. She thought: how could I let this be happening? She thought: what if I never feel this ever again?

And then she quit trying to think, because nothing seemed to make sense but his scent, his touch, the textures and sounds of Andy. His palms made slow, sweeping circles under her sweater, her bare skin igniting where he touched, his mouth caressing a smooth, satin path down her throat. His fingers connected with her bra.

She never felt the hooks give, yet her breasts suddenly felt freer, less tight and aching. His hands continued to roam her back, but they'd move, she knew. Her breasts hurt, as if they already knew what it was to be touched by Andy. He'd take off her sweater. He'd touch her. It was just the waiting that had her nervous, the terribly vulnerable feeling of urgency. She kissed him back, aware she'd been kissing him back for surely hours now, that Andy couldn't doubt her willingness. From the heat and emotion pouring off him, she couldn't doubt his.

The heels of his palms slid to her side, his touch lightening, gentling. Fingertips traced her ribs. A thumb edged up, almost, not quite, touching her breast. Anticipation burned through her like a streak of fire.

Slower than liquid gold, his mouth lifted from hers. His cheek nuzzled against her cheek, while they both gasped

in air. His hand, his warm, hot, big hand, rested for another second on her bare rib cage. And then dropped.

He smoothed her sweater down.

Down. Not up.

Her eyes shot open in confusion. His face was right
there, his dark eyes like wet ebony, grave in their intensity, none of that drawling, lazy humor of his anywhere
near that expression. But his tenor was softer than a velvet
whisper. "I had this bad feeling the minute I laid eyes on
you that you were going to be trouble for me, Maggie."

"You're blaming me for this trouble?"

"Uh-huh." There came that slow smile of his. "Of
course this is only a first pounce. Not like we've singed
our fingers near real fire yet."

Maybe he hadn't. She sure as shootin' had.

He reached for his jacket. "The only afternoon I've got
free this week is Thursday. You want to try something
nice and safe—and cold—like cross-country skiing?"

Maggie watched him pull out of the drive with her arms
hugged tight across her chest, feeling bemused and wondrous and all shook up.

That was a low-down thing he'd done—teasing her
with those kisses, clipping off the embrace after arousing
her to the point of frustration. The odd thing was…it made
her feel wooed. She didn't know a man who wouldn't
have pushed for a yes when things had gone that far. Just
possibly Andy thought they had something worth building, something worth risking more than instant fast sex.

When his car lights disappeared, she pivoted. There
seemed to be a hundred lights to turn off, the house to
lock up, and then Cleopatra's nose was pressed to the
glass doors on the porch. The raccoon was waiting for her
nightly handout of carrots and salad scraps. As Maggie

closed down for the night, she informed herself—firmly—
that she wasn't falling in love with him.

Maybe his kisses tipped the lid on her sanity. Maybe
she thought he was an incredibly special man. But she
was way too practical and grounded to believe anyone
could fall in love—serious love—that quickly. And besides that, he scared her.

She didn't know how he was doing that goofy magic
thing but it worried her. Self-reliance was her theme song.
She'd just never been the type of woman to run around,
humming arias with a delicious, giddy rush in her pulse.
There had to be a catch.

A few minutes later, as she climbed into bed and snuggled in, she was still struggling to analyze what the catch
might be. So far she hadn't seen any terrifying problems
in Andy. So far she hadn't found one reason why it wasn't
okay to be downright thrilled she was going to see him
again.

But a few hours later, she woke from a sound sleep in
her pitch-dark bedroom. Her palms were sticky with
sweat, her heart hammering, her pulse racing, racing with
an overwhelming feeling of anxiety.

It was just like all the other nights since the accident.
There was no specific dream or nightmare she remembered, nothing to explain this crushing feeling that
she'd done something wrong. Not failed-to-pay-a-bill or
bumped-a-fender wrong. But something serious, something real, that festered in her conscience like a sharp
prickly bush.

She'd racked her brain dozens of times, trying to remember the day of the accident. Nothing came. Nothing.
It was like those twenty-four hours starting with Thanksgiving dinner had never happened. For Pete's sake.
Whether or not she could recall the events, Maggie knew

positively that she'd had dinner with her sister and the boys. Gone home. Probably worked on the computer the next morning. It just seemed impossible that she could have done anything to earn this kind of soul-troubling guilt.

But it refused to go away.

Because her heart was still pounding, she reached over and fumbled for the bedside lamp. Yellow light immediately pooled on the disgraceful clutter all over her bedroom loft. The distracted thought popped in her head that she simply couldn't have Andy sleep here until she'd cleaned the place up.

And then she squeezed her eyes closed. Okay, okay, so she was thinking about making love with Andy. Not immediately. Still, if the relationship kept building the way it had been, Maggie couldn't deny that hopes for a serious future had sneaked into her thoughts.

Only these anxiety attacks of hers *were* the catch between them. Rushing into the relationship was a mistake. Andy valued integrity. Honesty. Cripes, he couldn't be a lawman without a strong moral and ethical code. But those values she respected were the precise reason she needed to be cautious.

If she'd done something seriously wrong, she needed to *know*. For her sake, but for his, too. Some mistakes, Andy could well find difficult to forgive or understand.

She simply *had* to do something to make herself remember those lost twenty-four hours.

Five

Two mornings later, Maggie could have sworn the world was coming up roses. For the first time since the accident, she'd wakened up raring to go, no longer wincing from the bumps and bruises. The day's agenda was strictly play, shopping with her sister this morning and skiing with Andy this afternoon. The sun was brilliant, the air so fresh it burned her lungs, and she and Joanna had found a parking place—a near miracle with all the bustling, hustling shoppers on Main Street.

As she pushed open the door to Mulliker's, her sister was still cheerfully chattering ten for a dozen about their shopping venture. Inside it was blessedly warm, the familiar department store all decked out with holiday trimmings, from twinkling lights to a roly-poly Santa in the lobby. Yet from absolutely nowhere, Maggie suddenly felt a shiver of anxiety skate up her spine.

Joanna was just unzipping her jacket. "Hey, what's wrong?"

"Nothing," Maggie assured her with a swift smile, but on the inside, she wanted to kick herself in the keister. Everything was fine. There was no excuse for giving in to this stomach-clenching, heart-pounding nonsense. The nightmares were bad enough, but there couldn't possibly be anything in the store to bring on that lead-weight guilty feeling, and she was determined to make this an upbeat morning for her sister. Joanna loved shopping, and for the first time in a long time, her sis was looking animated and all charged up and even pink-cheeked. "Where do you want to head first, Jo? Clothes for the boys?"

"Yeah—although I'm not sure about doing more than window shopping here. Maybe we should drive to Boulder for the day. Mulliker's is so expensive, Mags."

"We can do a day in Boulder next week if you want. But we might as well check out the home ground first." Mulliker's was the best store in White Branch. Maggie didn't care about the expense; she cared that the store catered to the labels and styles teenagers loved. Again, her heart started pounding as they ambled into the clothes section for teenage boys, but again, impatiently, Maggie sloughed it off. She zeroed quickly on a table of sweaters and held one up to show her sister. "You think Rog'd go for this?"

Joanna did, until she searched out the price tag. "Forget it. That's way too much."

"Sheesh, that's the whole point. That's what aunts get to do at Christmas time—buy loot the kids normally couldn't afford. And preferably something their parents don't want them to have."

"Yeah, I remember the set of drums you got when the

boys were toddlers. You're lucky I didn't murder you at the time.''

Maggie laughed. "You *still* holding a grudge?"

"Heavens, no. I just like Ivana's philosophy of life— don't get mad, get even. Which means I'm waiting until you have kids. As fast as they come out of the womb, I'm buying them percussion instruments.''

"You wouldn't do that to me," Maggie informed her. "Now let's get serious here, what's on your list?"

"Jeans, underwear, socks, long johns..." Joanna had been so peppy and cheerful, but her face suddenly fell. "I swear they seem to need everything. Both of them are just growing like weeds—and I see that look on your face, Mags. No. I'm not taking any more money from you, so don't even try and offer. I haven't even started repaying the last money you gave me—''

"That wasn't a loan, you goose. That's something already forgotten and was never missed. I keep telling you, I'm getting a great salary that I can't possibly spend just on myself. Frankly, I'd like to get the kids a computer. That cranky old thing they've been trying to use—''

"No." Joanna parked in front of a sale rack of sweatshirts. "I need to get a job. To get my life back together. I know that, Maggie, I just wish to Pete I had an ounce of your kind of strength.''

"You're strong. You've just had a huge traumatic thing to handle this last year." While Joanna was distracted, Maggie plucked two shirts off the rack and buried the sweater underneath. "Nobody's strong all the time.''

"You are. And I don't want you overspending on us this time. You just had to buy a car.''

"That was no sweat. I had great collision insurance. Ended up practically ahead on the deal." That wasn't strictly true, but Joanna had never had the financial sense of a kumquat. It was her sister's fragility and whole ethereal spirit that had Maggie so concerned about her.

"Speaking of collisions…you didn't tell me how that outing went with the sheriff. Are you going to see him again?"

"Uh-huh. In fact we're going cross-country skiing this afternoon." When her sister abandoned another shirt because of price, Maggie hurled it under the growing load in her arms.

"Linda says every matchmaker in town has tried to set him up since his divorce."

"Is this Linda the hairdresser or Linda the bank teller we're quoting?"

"Linda the hairdresser, naturally. You know she knows everything that happens in White Branch. His ex-wife was named Dianne. She was really beautiful, they say."

"Yeah? You think Rog'd go for this?" Maggie held up a Denver Broncos sweatshirt.

"Is a rabbi Jewish? They were married five years. He met her on some ski trip. The way it sounds, she did one of those women routines—said she loved everything he did, claimed to share his interests? Then they got married. All the outside sports he loved, she hated. She'd told him small towns were just her cuppa, then moved here and whined about being stifled. Linda said he drank quite a bit when she first left him."

"The way you're describing it, I'd have drunk quite a bit when she was still there," Maggie retorted.

"He quit that. Then started going out. Linda said he's probably been out with every single woman in a three-county radius."

"Is there some reason Linda volunteered all this gossip about Andy's private life out of the total blue?" Maggie added socks and T-shirts to the growing pile in her arms.

"Well, sure. I asked her. If you're thinking about getting involved with this guy, I wanted the inside information. Nobody's caught him, Mags, and a lot of women have tried. Maybe he picked up an allergy to commitment after his first marriage."

"Maybe he did. Maybe I would, too, after an experience like that. I always hated that 'catching a man' thing. It always sounds like a woman's trying to lasso a prize horse. The way you described it, she wasn't honest with him. Or herself. No wonder it ended up a disaster. Why can't couples just be straight with each other?"

"Because it goes against all the laws of civilization," Joanna announced, and then shook her head when she saw Maggie's heaped arms. "We've got to quit before we've bought out the store."

"Okay, but do the kids need coats?"

"Yeah, but what they've got'll do for one more winter season."

En route to the cash register, though, Maggie spotted a rack of leather bomber jackets. Colin'd die for one, she knew…and that thought barely surfaced before she suffered another palm-dampening clutch of anxiety. Damnation. She simply had to get control over this dumb thing. "Joanna?"

"What?"

"Did anything weird happen on Thanksgiving?"

"You're still letting that bug you? Maggie, that's silly. Probably the only reason you can't remember is because you started worrying about not being able to."

"That's probably true. But all the same—was something different about that holiday dinner?" Other customers were hovering at the cash register. Maggie heaped all the clothes in her sister's arms so she could dig out the credit card from her purse.

"No, of course not. It was just a Thanksgiving. We had turkey, Mom's cranberry-orange salad. I burned the rolls. Nothing new—except that was the night my oldest devil son started turning into an angel. You talked to Colin, in fact, for quite a long time outside on the back porch."

Maggie looked up. "Do you know what we talked about?"

"I assume about shaping up his act. You know what a wild crowd he's been taking up with. They all drink and have too much money. And if he'd skipped school one more time, he was risking suspension…" Joanna sighed. "Whatever you said seemed to suddenly turn him around. Maggie, you've been counseling both boys since their dad died. Doing a far better job being their mom than I am—"

"Joanna, that's not true! You're a wonderful mom!"

"I used to think I was," Joanna said fretfully. "But not lately. I get worried and nervous and then I yell. I know they're not listening to me, not like they do to you—hey!"

"Hey what?" Their turn had come up at the cash register. Maggie'd already heaped the clothes on the counter and handed over her card.

"Maggie, you're not paying for all my stuff and yours, too! We need to sort out what's what—"

"It's just not worth all that hassle with a whole line of people behind us," Maggie said smoothly. "Let me just pay. It'll be easier. And you can settle up with me later."

Her sister would forget about settling up later, Maggie suspected, which was fine—except that sneaking her sis some financial help seemed worth no more than putting a Band Aid on a broken leg. Joanna's increasing lack of confidence not only alarmed her, but made her feel impotent and helpless—alien emotions to Maggie.

As they left the store, though, her mind spun ahead to

the afternoon coming with Andy. Between worrying about her sister and those aggravating anxiety attacks, she really hadn't felt like herself since the accident. Her whole life just seemed all shook up lately.

Except for him. Maybe Andy was shaking her up, too, but that was because he was the one thing in her life that was unexpectedly—downright deliriously—wonderful.

When Andy knocked on Maggie's door, it was past five o'clock. Just a wee bit late—considering he was supposed to pick her up at three.

Her yard light was on. No surprise. The sun had long disappeared and the moon hadn't shown her face yet, so that the whole landscape looked dunked in darkness. When Maggie didn't immediately answer, he rapped again, then stepped back and rolled his shoulders to shake out the kinks from a long, tedious, pit-awful day. Her new vehicle was parked in the drive, so she was home. But whether she was willing to answer a date this wincingly late was still a question.

Andy raised his knuckles one more time—just as her back door hurled open. She was suddenly there, like a blast of sunshine. He took her in in a gulp, from the snuggly yellow sweater to the skinny jeans to the hair bouncing around her shoulders. His heart felt sucker-punched even before he caught the warm, welcoming light in her eyes. The smile was more frosting—he'd been so sure she'd be ticked off.

"Maggie, I'm really sorry—"

"So you said twice on the answering machine. I got the messages, Andy, it's okay." She ushered him in, shutting out the cold and the whole bleak evening. "You didn't explain on the messages, but I figured you must have had a problem at work?"

"Yeah." He wasn't about to tell her how a simple traffic violation had turned up a trunkful of militia-type weapons. He'd brought in the state guys himself, but nothing ever went fast once those boys poked their noses in. The jerk had been removed from his territory now, but the whole day had been an exhausting wipeout.

"You look really beat," Maggie said sympathetically.

Well, he had been. Until she impulsively reached up, with a quick squeeze of his arm and a peck that wouldn't quite pass as a kiss—but she'd still volunteered it. And he'd still been half expecting some kind of female blistering scold. His ex-wife would have scrubbed the floor with him for being so late and screwing up plans. So would half the women he knew.

She rocked back down on her heels swiftly. Like before, she'd shown nerves that he might misunderstand an affectionate gesture. Andy understood perfectly well that she meant no come-on, just some empathy, but damn. It should be gone by now. That electric charge from just being near her. The wallop of testosterone. The sudden heel-clicking vibrant feeling that the whole world had turned right because he was with her.

There just *had* to be a glitch. She couldn't be this perfect. For him. With him. For Pete's sake, they still barely knew each other.

"You're being awfully understanding...considering a mangy guy showed up at your door, unshaved and unbrushed, who totally blew our daylight hours for cross-country skiing."

"I see the whiskers. But this is probably one of those toothpaste things—if you show up looking a little mangy, then I don't have to be embarrassed if I have a hole in a sock. And as far as the original plans...when I realized you were going to be tied up, I came up with another idea. But are you still on call?''

''Technically my Thursday afternoon and night's free, but how it really works—especially today—is that I'm off. As long as I can be reached by cell phone.''

She propped her hands on her hips. ''So...I can basically kidnap you—as long as you can call home?''

''Now there's a tricky question to ask a lawman—but the answer isn't. You, Maggie, can kidnap me on any terms you want,'' he said wryly.

Of course, he didn't actually think she meant it.

An hour later, he'd suffered through some intensive experiences as a kidnappee...and enjoyed every minute of it.

They'd skied a mile from her house, watching the full moon rise right ahead of them. He'd played pack mule. The mysterious supplies she'd stuffed in his backpack weighed up, but nothing to distract him from the pleasures of the trek. The hike was just long enough to chase away the day's stresses. The moonlight on snow was another world, breath-stealing and peaceful, with the surrounding pine woods rustling scents and whispering shadows. They'd scared up a deer—then a fox—but no wildlife had intruded on their privacy in a while now.

A mesmerizing fire snapped and crackled in a stone-circle bed, but Andy's gaze kept drifting to the far more mesmerizing view of Maggie. She was hunched over, basting the chicken hanging from a makeshift spit of sticks. She'd carried the kindling. He'd been carrying the chicken, a flask of hot mulled cider and foil-wrapped potatoes. While she worked, he endured the exhausting role of captive, using a giant log as a backrest and stretched out on a blanket she'd brought.

The knoll was out of sight from her house—an ideal

hideaway if he'd ever seen one. It looked over a sharp ravine, with the glisten of water below, gushing against virgin-white snowbanks. The moon peeked between mountain breasts.

"You've got a piece of heaven here," he remarked.

"Don't I know it. The beauty back here is what sold me on the property, but thankfully you can't see how special it is from the road. I have a terror some darn fool tourists are going to find it sometime and do some horrible thing like try to develop it. Uh-oh—you know what? I forgot glasses."

"I believe we'll survive, sharing a flask. For one thing, I'm pretty sure the potency of that cider would scare off any germs we even tried to share."

She turned around with a grin. "Like it? It has to brew for some hours with a bunch of spices. It doesn't really have that much alcohol, but it sure seems to have a kick on a cold night."

He hadn't noticed any cold. Her knoll opened onto the view of the ravine, but tall pines flanked the secluded spot from the backside, blocking any hint of wind, sheltering them and the toasty fire both. Still, the warmth she generated was the heat he noticed most. "You know, Killer, I insulted you before for being a total failure as a potential criminal. But I take it back. You have some real planning and organizational skills as a kidnapper. Maybe there's a future for you behind bars yet."

"Yeah, well, you're big on the compliments now, but you haven't sampled my cooking yet. The chicken's definitely ready. No, don't get up. You're the one who had the hard day."

Andy had no objections to being spoiled, but slowly he discovered that her day had hardly been a prizewinner, either. Nothing, no caviar or gourmet French cooking, could possibly have tasted as succulent as that fire-braised chicken. Maggie settled next to him, sharing the blanket, and both fell on the food like ravenous wolves. When she started telling him about Christmas shopping with her sister that morning, Andy understood that she meant just lighthearted chatter—but her worries about her sister easily seeped through in her tone and her eyes.

"Maggie, it sounds like you feel responsible for their whole household," he remarked.

"Well...I do, in a way. With our parents gone, I'm all the family Joanna has. And after Steve died, she's just seemed increasingly lost. She was always an impractical dreamer, on the emotional, fragile side. And Steve tended to wrap her in cotton wool. She'd never balanced a checkbook, known how to fix a leaky faucet."

"You implied the oldest kid was in trouble? What kind of trouble?"

Maggie hesitated. "Colin...he's fifteen, the one you met the first day you stopped by the house. And I didn't mean real trouble, Andy. He's got a huge heart. He was always the mischievous one, but after his dad died, it was like he felt angry, confused. Got into some fights, took up with some kids on the wild side, skipped school. Nothing that bad—he doesn't have a mean bone in his body. He just..."

Andy filled in the blank. "He wanted his dad back."

Maggie nodded. "And Joanna's been so wrapped up in her own grief. It's not like she doesn't love them more than life. But she just doesn't want to hear a problem. Even little things really throw her."

Andy leaned over, giving their silverware and plates a wash in the snow. The cleanup took a whole two minutes. "Joanna seemed pretty together the night I met her, Maggie. She looked me over pretty good once she realized

this strange man in the driveway was coming to see her
younger sister. Thought for a second I was going to have
to provide references and credentials both,'' he said
wryly.

"Men usually take one look at her and fall like nine-
pins," Maggie said. "The blond hair and big eyes?"

Andy'd seen the blond hair and big eyes. And Maggie's
sister was unquestionably attractive, but it seemed recently the only standard of female beauty that pushed his
buttons had shoulder-length brown hair and distinctly
green eyes. More to the immediate point, he'd garnered
an increasingly clear picture of the rescuer role Maggie
had taken in the family. Chores, money, time, caretaking
the boys... "Sometimes, you have to give someone a reason to stand on their own feet, Mags," he said carefully.

"But she's never been really responsible—"

"Maybe she could be?"

"Well, yeah. Maybe. But what if she needed me and I
wasn't there?"

Clearly walking through fire was a preferable option to
failing her sister in any way. Andy suspected there was
no point arguing with that fierce loyalty of hers, and since
he didn't really know the situation, he had no business
intruding besides. He finished putting away the supplies,
added a few more sticks to the fire, and then crashed down
beside her again. "Come here, you."

"Come where?"

He snuggled her up in the curve of his shoulder.
"You're going to have to suffer through a hug. It's about
that mean, cold heart of yours, Killer. I keep finding out
things about you that just really turn me off."

"Yeah, I can see how you're turned off. I keep warning
you, Gautier, don't start thinking I'm a nice person."

Considering they had a good five pounds of bulky winter clothes between them, it was downright amazing a simple hug could inspire any feeling of intimacy. Maybe it was the way she cuddled up, fitting against him like the missing half of his puzzle piece. Or those luminous green eyes, tipped to his, so full of the devil...but aware of him, too.

"Nice person? Are you kidding? I never thought any such thing. In my job, you have to develop a tough, fast judgment of character or you just couldn't survive. I took one look at you in that hospital bed and realized right off what a wicked woman you were. Speaking of which... have you remembered that lost twenty-four hours yet?" The question made her go oddly still, so Andy could see it was still bugging her.

"No."

"Well, I don't think it's hard to guess the kind of seven deadly sins you've been up to. Hell, you could have been tried and convicted of gluttony and kidnapping just in the last couple hours."

"You're accusing *me* of greed? The way you inhaled enough dinner for three men?"

"Hey, we're not talking about my sins. We're talking about yours. And somehow I think this conversation's gonna lag real quick because you won't be able to come up with a list."

"I certainly can. I'll have you know I'm a thief."

"Yeah?" He brushed a strand of hair from her cheek, not too impressed with this confession so far.

"I stole Mrs. Meglethorn's raspberries from her back-yard when I was six. More than once. And furthermore— oh man, I do love raspberries—I'd probably do it again."

"Holy cow. I'm shocked. Who'd have guessed you'd commit a sin of that magnitude? I should have brought my handcuffs."

"Now, don't you start with those handcuff threats, Gautier."

He didn't. But he gave her a kiss because she was sure as hell asking for one. Her face was tilted up to his, catching the glow of firelight, her lips parting to meet his even before he'd ducked down. She tasted winsome and wicked-soft. She tasted like the woman he'd been missing all his life. She tasted like the magic he'd never really dared believe in. But something in his technique must have been missing, because she interrupted the kiss to mutter, "Pride."

"Pride? Ah...you're trying to distract me back to the deadly sin track again?" Considering she was breathless and her cheeks still flushed from that kiss, Andy didn't figure that her mind was entirely on that past conversation. But she obviously didn't want to let go until she'd cleared up any wild misconceptions he could be harboring about her being a good woman.

"I'm not sure I remember all the sins on that list. There's gluttony, sloth, envy, anger...but I'm pretty sure pride's in there somewhere. A few times—like when I was determined to do the Appalachian Trail alone? That may have been a little, very slightly, just a teensy bit, dumb."

"You got hurt, did you?" His thumb traced the soft underside of her jaw.

"Not hurt, but I got caught in a shelter one night with some guys. They'd been drinking and as soon as I realized that, I should have moved on. It turned out okay, but maybe if I hadn't been so egotistical to think I could handle anything alone, I wouldn't have walked into that one. And another time, I was doing some mountain climbing...really just exercises. But I knew better than to do that alone, too. Fell, cracked an ankle. It was really stupid."

"Sounds it," he agreed.

Her eyebrows feathered up. "Hey...I thought you'd be good for some sympathy."

"Nope. Those sound like sins of pride to me, too. Being a perfect human being myself, of course, I've never done anything that dumb. Even when I rode a dirt cycle into the mountains one day, got caught in a snowstorm, damn near broke my neck—but that was a different thing. I wasn't dumb. The weather was dumb."

"Ah." Her eyes were dancing. "I should have guessed you'd understand, Andy."

"About the need to challenge and push your limits sometimes? To test what you're made of? Maybe to court just a little danger?" Andy grinned. "Yeah. I've been there, done that, and paid all the prices. But back to the subject at hand. There are two more on that deadly sins list you haven't gotten to yet."

"What?"

"Damned if I know. But lust has to be one. Lust is always on somebody's bad list. You want to talk about that?"

"Um...no."

Neither did he. Talking was never half as much fun as doing. And her arm was already reaching around his neck to pull him down.

Six

Since Maggie seemed determined to confess all the terrible sins in her past—and prove to him once and for all that she was no kin to a good woman—Andy wasn't sure what motivated the sudden change in her mood. When she looped an arm around his neck to volunteer a kiss, though, he was way too much of a gentleman to fight her off.

Another place, another time, he might have worried about consequences. But right then, the chill of deep night was starting to seriously settle in, and the fire had died down too far to provide warmth for much longer. He wasn't about to risk frostbite on her tush, hadn't brought protection—so many safety factors were built in that there was simply no reason not to indulge in a kiss. Or ten.

Her lips were soft and smooth but ice-cold.

That wasn't a problem for long.

She was smiling one of those full-of-the-female-devil

smiles when they started—possibly because of his teasing about her lurid, sinful past. He loved the smile, but that didn't last long either.

Since that first kiss only seemed to frustrate her, he angled down for another. This one involved tongues and teeth, and seemed to do a far better job of inspiring her concentration. Her eyes turned lustrous, vulnerable. And her arms suddenly tightened around his neck, her fingers clutching and clenching as if wary he'd disappear on her.

He wasn't going anywhere.

The log they'd been using as a backrest was in the way. He scootched her down to the blanket, angling his thigh between hers, deepening a kiss that was already plumbing the depths for trouble. He wanted to give her trouble. More trouble than she could handle—a daunting task when they were both wearing so much winter gear that hands and faces were the only body parts exposed.

But it was all Maggie's fault he was provoked into trying. Andy fully realized he was already in trouble over his head. Everything about her drew him. Her stubborn independent streak. Her gutsy spirit. Her unyielding integrity. He'd uncovered some flaws, thank God. He loved her loyalty to her sis and family, but for her own sake, he thought she took it too far. She had zero patience with life chores she hated—like car shopping—and tended to dive off a cliff to get them over with. And she took some risks that were dangerously unwise, like her solo Appalachian Trail hike. Except for those personal little quirks, though, Andy hadn't seen much reason why Maggie would invite a man into her life.

So far, that was the only terrorizing glitch he'd found in Maggie—she was so strong and self-reliant that she just didn't seem to need a mate. Weeks ago, he could have related to that completely, because he'd never particularly felt the wolf-howl loneliness for a mate before himself. But he did now. The hunger to love had never sucked him under until Maggie. He'd never felt so much, so bewilderingly fast. The power of chemistry was so sharp it clawed at him with hot, biting teeth. He was wary of believing anything this perfect—yet the whole world changed colors when he was with her, and for double damn sure when he touched her.

He feared he was alone on that island, that Maggie wasn't in half as much emotional trouble as he was...but things sure did change when he kissed her.

He couldn't fathom it. It wasn't as though Maggie's gutsy confidence disappeared when his arms were around her. But she knew him now. Knew how he tasted, knew how he kissed, so he kept thinking that stunned, volatile responsiveness of hers would fade by now. Instead her expression, in the glow of firelight, had turned fragile and vulnerable. Her lips met his, matching the pressure and tension of his kisses, as if this were all breathlessly new and she was tremblingly unprepared. She turned liquid for him, with him.

It was a dangerous thing to do to a guy's ego. Make him feel like he was the only man who'd ever been in her universe.

He captured her hands, pulled them over her head...not exerting any real control over her in any way. Just playing. Just...seeing. If Maggie liked that sensation of yielding and giving someone else the nasty responsibility of control once in a while.

Dynamite was less volatile. She made a soft, throaty groan, buried between kisses, and her long legs twisted around him, her pelvis rocking evocatively against his. She tugged, wanting her hands freed, and he freed them...just as soon as he'd gotten around to kissing her hot and senseless. The blanket beneath them bunched and tangled. Their ski pants and jackets slip-slided, the bulky fabrics in their way, and the fire was spitting too damn close. Still, his tongue dived in her mouth, mimicking love play. And he saw her eyes in the firelight, lost and smoky, as she kissed back with abandon.

Maybe she'd loved. But he was starting to feel reassurance that he wasn't the only one in trouble. He wasn't alone falling off this cliff. No woman had ever looked at him the way she did. No woman had responded to him with this kind of earthy, honest, pure sensual vulnerability. She wasn't…afraid. More as though surprise circumvented her natural defenses. She just wasn't used to two people being able to generate a cataclysmic earthquake with a few basic kisses.

Hell, neither was he. And teasing her was important, Andy sensed. He intuited that just maybe, no man had. Maggie was too strong to be happy about relinquishing control. Sex was a whole lot easier if you just scratched the itch, got it over with, didn't have to risk too much. But it was a hunger to love driving him, not just sex, and he didn't want her just scratching an itch with him. He wanted her trust, and that simply couldn't be won fast, not with her, never with her. Meanness was called for. He was inspired to make her miserable, make her…testy. Arousing frustration in Maggie just might open up those doors to trust.

He was pretty sure that basic theory was dead right.

There was just a slight problem with application.

When the blanket tugged and snarled again, her head dipped back against the white snow. He rolled, carrying her with him so she was on top. If one of them was going catch their death with a snow-wet head, it wasn't going to be her.

"Andy..." She took to being on top as explosively as she had to being on the bottom. Sanity was slipping away from him in fistfuls. He informed himself that he'd always had mountains of patience, especially as a lover. Always. No exceptions.

"Andy..." She framed his face, taking kisses, her full weight pressed on him as if she was savoring torturing him half to death. Eventually she tried talking again, although her voice was as hoarse as a whisper. "Come on, we have to stop this. We both know this is nuts. It's late. The fire's almost gone. We're going to freeze to death."

"Uh-huh. Well, I hate to be the one to tell you this, Mags, but you're the one kissing me."

"Shut up and open your jacket, Gautier."

He shut up and unzipped her jacket. Then his. There still seemed to be five thousand pounds of fabric between them, but it helped. There had to be enough body heat crushed between her breasts and his chest to melt an avalanche. Or two.

His sanity slipped another notch. Hell, it fell straight down a bottomless well. Winning her trust was a serious thing. It just seemed like he could work on that tomorrow. Right then he wanted her naked on a hard mattress behind a locked door, preferably ten minutes ago. He could feel the shape of her breasts, but not touch them. He could feel the curve of her hips through ski pants and jeans, but he couldn't touch that smooth, soft, supple skin. He wanted flesh. He wanted her. And the desire spearing through him burned like a sharp-hot ache.

"Andy...we could—"

"Dammit, Maggie, don't tell me that."

Her hair was all tumbled, glowing like golden cognac in the firelight. Her wet red mouth was trembly now, and those deep soft eyes of hers reflected both desire—and honesty. "I'm not sure it's right. I'm scared it's too soon, but Andy...I've just never felt like this. With anyone. And I can't believe it's wrong, not with feelings this strong—"

A discordant sound came from nowhere. All kinds of noises surrounded them—the rustling of pines, a whistling wind, the hiss of a dying fire. But those were all natural sounds, unlike the confounded civilized intrusion of a telephone ringing.

Maggie's head jerked up as if someone had slapped her. "That has to be your cell phone in the backpack?"

He muttered, "Yes," accompanied by a creative selection of cuss words. And then he kissed her again.

"Someone could be in trouble. Don't you really have to answer it?"

He muttered, "Dammit, yes, I have to answer it." But he gave her one more slam of a kiss before detangling their bodies and stalking over to the damn cell phone in the damn backpack. The only voice he wanted to hear was Maggie's. And he *really* wanted to hear where she was taking that conversation—not that his hormones weren't already drumbeating that answer.

She was willing. They could have made love. Not conveniently or easily, but Maggie seemed more than up for a fast, furious wild adventure in the snow. And so was he.

But the law, unfortunately, was his life as well as his job. Reception on the cell phone was fuzzy, but Andy could make out the problem well enough. Paul Shonefeld was tearing up Babe's bar—not for the first time—but knives had shown up in the fight. His part-time deputy knew damn well Andy'd kill him if he'd tried to tackle that kind of problem solo.

Maggie only had to hear his end of the conversation to

shoot to her feet. By the time he'd severed the call, she'd already tended to the fire and was folding up the blanket.

Within minutes, they were speed-skiing back to her house. Their race in the bitter wind should have clipped those drumbeating hormones of his, but somehow it didn't work that way. The thing was, Maggie had not only efficiently packed them up, but said nothing at all. His ex-wife would have expected two weeks of apologies and gone on about his job being more important than her. Maggie just seemed to accept and understand that his work didn't fit into a neat nine-to-five pigeonhole.

Back at her place, he hustled the gear inside, then leaned her up against the shadows of the back door for one last, long kiss. "Now, that's much better, Gautier," she murmured.

"Better?" He didn't know what she meant.

"Yeah. Your smile's back. I thought you were gonna bark my head off for a little while there."

"I was never mad at you, Maggie."

"I know. You were mad at the interruption. But that scowl of yours was still darker than a thundercloud." She hesitated. "I know you have to go. I just have to say…this didn't quite work out like we planned. Somehow I thought a nice, healthy, wholesome little cookout was a safe thing to do together."

"So did I. Only snow and cold didn't even seem to slow us down, Killer. Maybe we should try swimming in a mountain lake in a blizzard?"

"You think that'd work better?"

He touched her cheek. "No. I think we both know where this is headed. But the last thing I want to do is rush you, Maggie. We'll find a way to slow this down."

Andy meant it when he said it, but *how* was the question.

* * *

When he finally pulled into the parking lot at Babe's bar, Mavis was waiting for him. His part-time deputy was forty-seven, black-haired, black-eyed, and a wiry half-pint at five foot four. Unlike John, who had the size but neither the skill nor the guts, Mavis could probably have leveled any man in the fight—without getting winded—but Andy was rigid on certain safety policies. There were situations they weren't to touch without backup, and this was one of them.

A gunshot got the crowd's attention, possibly because the brawlers had already worn themselves out partying. After that, there was just doing what had to be done. The bar was good and torn up, broken chairs, a shattered mirror, a table overturned...but the people damages were worse. One guy's arm was seriously cut; another man was clean knocked out; three or four others were bruised up. Paul Shonefeld had thrown the first punch, nothing new. Paul was born with a bully streak and liquor only made him meaner. He always had enough money to pay the damages and skate by on misdemeanors.

Not this time. Andy had Mavis cart two to the hospital to get the cuts sewn up, heard Babe rant and rave until he was pacified, yelled at the crowd to get on home, and then trundled a drunken Paul into his car. Shonefeld predictably stank of cheap rye and sweat, and bitched like a belligerent bull the whole ride to the jail.

Andy didn't argue, just took him in. The law shared building space with the post office. On their side, the front office held three utilitarian desks; beyond that was a side room for meetings and interrogations. Except for a bathroom, there was only one other room in the back—not really a jail, but a cubicle with barred windows, a single cot and a door with a steel lock. Paul knew the way. The county had put him up at taxpayers' expense before.

"I'll be out by tomorrow," he blustered.

"Nope, you won't. You crossed the line when you drew a knife."

"I didn't draw the first knife. It was Booker. I was just defending myself. Nobody can say otherwise—"

"I'm saying otherwise, Shonefeld. Now you got water, you got a john, and I don't want to hear another peep out of you until morning. Anything else you can tell the judge."

"I get my phone call first—"

Technically, he had that right, but he also passed out on the cot before anyone could have obliged him. By then it was way after midnight, but naturally, there was confounded paperwork to fill out for the report.

Andy settled in his grandaddy-sized office chair, the neon office light beaming lonely on his head. Christmas lights lit up Main Street, but not a single car passed by this late. The only sounds in the place were the ticking clock and his pen scratching on paper.

It always took a while for the adrenaline to pump back down after handling someone like Shonefeld, but his mind wasn't on the fracas. Maggie seeped back in his thoughts. Subzero on a blizzardy night after a two hour altercation with the ugly side of his job, and still she was there, sneaking into his mind like the drifting scent of roses on a sultry summer night.

She was good. That was part of it. Andy knew a ton of good people, but he also knew that a strong, pure, giving heart like hers was a rare thing—worth treasuring the same as a fragile rose. Temporarily, though, it wasn't exactly Maggie's goodness that had his mind spinning at a hundred miles an hour.

Pictures played in his head. Slow-motion, fantasizing, tantalizing pictures of a wild, wicked fling in the snowy woods with her. He couldn't stop thinking that another time, it could have happened. That he wanted it to happen. But—at least in theory—it'd been damn lucky it hadn't happened tonight.

His hormones had gotten ahead of him, when he'd already given himself the stern lecture about going slow with her. Their evening together had only further underlined how important that was. The rightness he felt with Maggie was too special to risk blowing. That she chose to live alone told him clearly that other guys had either let her down or tried to tie her down.

Andy wanted to do neither. But if Maggie saw love as a noose instead of as a source of freedom, he obviously needed time to show her a relationship could be different than what she feared.

He'd never met a woman who seemed more perfect for him. A soul mate like he'd never believed could exist. Andy suddenly tossed down his pen and squeezed his eyes closed, impatiently aware that he was trying to strategize behavior that would win Maggie. You couldn't strategize magic. He couldn't even explain why she was such magic for him.

But she was.

And his heart already knew it.

Maggie yanked on her jacket, grabbed a ladder and stomped outside. The sun was so blinding bright that the snow looked like a rolling carpet of diamonds. As far as she was concerned, the breathtaking landscape could go hang. Her mood rivaled a grumpy grizzly bear's. A female bear. With P.M.S.

She stabbed the ladder into a two-foot snowbank and braced the top against the eaves. Stomped back in the garage for a tub of tar and a spatula. Carted those supplies back to the ladder. Then dropped the supplies and stood with hands on hips, squinting up at the steep edge of her roof.

This was all Andy's fault. Well, not the leak in her roof. The first time she'd found a puddle on the bathroom floor was last summer, and she'd hired a roofer then to repair the problem. When she saw the fresh puddle this morning in exactly the same spot, she wanted to kick herself. How many times did she have to relearn the lesson that it was always a mistake to depend on anyone but yourself? Climbing up on a wet slippery roof in the dead of winter wasn't necessarily a real safe move, but Colorado was in for several heavy snow months. And that meant a heavy melt problem every time there was a blinding, brilliant sun like today. The damage could be serious if she waited until spring.

The leak wasn't Andy's fault. But her grizzly mood was. She was normally as even-tempered as a clam—except when she didn't get enough sleep. The nightmares plaguing her since the accident had practically quadrupled last night. And she'd decided Andy was responsible for those, too.

Her hiking boot skidded on the first ladder rung—but she steadied herself and tried again, balancing the tar and tools as she climbed to the top.

This magic thing was damned stupid. *Nobody* fell in love this fast. She'd practically thrown herself at him last night in the middle of the woods, for Pete's sake. Worse yet, it had seemed a perfectly natural and right thing to do at the time. Some nasty, dastardly thing was tricking her into believing she was head over heels in love with him, and the entire problem was making Maggie nervous. So nervous that she'd awakened over and over last night, with her heart slamming anxiety and her whole body shaking. She'd had it with the whole lost memory business. She'd racked and racked and racked her brain, trying to figure out what the Sam Hill she could conceivably have done to feel so guilty about. Flaws—cripes, she had character flaws up the wazoo. But she'd never done anything seriously outside her value system and couldn't imagine doing so.

Those dreams *must* have intensified because of Andy. He kept teasing her about being a good person. And she liked his teasing—she liked everything about the damn man—but his standard of ethics was as rigid as her own. And worrying that she might have done something to let Andy down or disappoint him had obviously bled into those troubling dreams.

She'd never had a problem with strength or self-control. That she couldn't slam a lid on those anxiety attacks shamed her—more so, because she didn't have a clue how to make them quit. Fixing the roof was at least a problem she could solve.

At least, that was the plan.

The ladder tried to tip when she reached the top rung. She gulped, then edged up and onto the roof itself. When building her cabin, she'd chosen the steepest roof slope possible—as would anyone with a brain living in this neck of the woods. This was a snowbelt. A sharp slope encouraged the snow to slide off. The risk of the roof crushing under the heavy weight of snow was lessened.

Only right now, that sharp slope meant tough climbing, and the relentlessly beating sun both helped and hurt her cause. Most of the snow had melted or fallen off, making this probably the only day all winter she could accomplish this leak fix. Only the sun had also created constant rivers of water and little icy patches. Her hiking boots provided good traction, but she was carrying the tar bucket, making any movement extra awkward.

"Hey, Maggie!"

Sheesh. She almost dropped the bucket and slid the whole length when she heard the sudden sound of a voice. She whipped her head around to see Colin. Her nephew had obviously spotted the ladder and climbed up to find her. His grin was full of the devil, his green eyes way too much like hers, and with the sun glinting on his face, she could easily spot the five whiskers on his chin that he was way too manly-proud to shave.

"You scared the holy hell out of me, you monster."

"Hey, you scared *me* when I saw you up here. How many times have you told me not to do stuff like this alone?"

"That's different. I'm the aunt. You're the kid. One of those cases where you're supposed to do what I say, not what I do." She swallowed hard when she looked down. "I really do need to get this done, but I don't know why you stopped by—if you need something, Colin—"

"No big deal. I was just gonna ask you what to get Mom for Christmas. And maybe getting out of the house for an hour seemed a good idea, too—"

Instantly Maggie picked up that cue. "Your mom having a rough day?"

"Yeah, kinda. First she got on Rog's case. Then she got on mine. Then she got upset at herself because she was on our cases. It's like, how do you win? You tell her okay, you'll do something, but it still doesn't make anything all right. But I didn't come here to talk about that. Look, I'll come up there and help you—"

"Hold it! No, Colin…" Holy cow, her nephew's comments already had her mind scuttling worries about Joanna's emotional fragility. But those worries paled when she saw Colin reaching for a grasp on the roof. "No, don't come up here! I mean it—in fact, I changed my mind about trying to do this and I'm coming down, too. It seemed a good idea to fix the leak because I knew exactly where the spot was, but it's just too darn slippery—"

"Don't sweat it. I got good boots. I'll just do it for you. It'd make me feel better, you know? Don't think I forgot how much I owe you, Mags. You shoulda called me, you needed some help. I'd have been over here in two shakes—"

The sudden color burning on his cheeks wasn't caused by the cold, and Maggie had no idea what the reference to his 'owing her' was about. Right then, though, there was no time to pursue any sideroad discussion. "No! Colin, I'm serious! Don't climb up here—it's not safe. I—oh, no. Oh, God."

Like a typical teenage boy, he'd vaulted up to the roof with athletic nimbleness. Only klutziness typically went with those teenage years too. His boot accidentally kicked at the top ladder rung. She saw the ladder tip and then crash sideways, out of sight. When Colin lost his foothold, he at least had the sense to plaster his body flat on the steep slope—safe enough. At least for that second.

"Oops," Colin said guiltily.

"Don't move, don't look, don't do anything." Maggie's voice automatically turned calm and take-charge cool. "Don't get shook up and do anything dumb. We're both fine, and we're both going to be fine. I'll find a way to get us down."

But when Maggie looked down, damned if she knew how they were going to manage it. She'd never been scared in a crisis, and resourcefulness was her middle name. But the ladder definitely wasn't reachable. And the two-story drop to the ground, even with snowdrifts possibly cushioning a jump, made the risk of injury serious—and out of the question for her nephew. Maggie'd shoot herself if Colin were hurt. And her sister would fall apart for sure if she even knew Colin were in this kind of danger.

"I'll find a way to get us down," she repeated reassuringly. "Just stay cool."

Being stranded on the roof was one problem, but keeping Colin from doing anything foolhardly was her first priority. A half hour later, Maggie had solved one crisis but not the second—when she saw the sheriff's car bounce into her driveway and brake with a screech.

Seven

"**W**hat the *hell* are you two doing?"

Given such a silly question—Andy could see perfectly well what they were doing—Maggie answered with the obvious. "Patching the roof. And actually, we're done. Hi, Andy."

"Hi, Killer. And hi…Colin, is it?"

"Yeah. Hi, Sheriff Gautier."

Maggie noticed that her nephew suddenly turned flush-faced and fidgety. The sheriff had a gift for making her nervous, too, but not likely for the same reasons. Since she and Colin were stranded on the roof, they'd gone ahead and patched the leak. Why not? They had nothing better to do until she conjured up some brilliant solution for how they were going to get down.

And Maggie had a plan. Fixing the roof had given her time to assess the situation and determine that there wasn't a brilliant solution in sight. She was going to have to jump. The west side of the house had both bushes and the highest snowdrifts—her best shot at cushioning her fall. The odds of a sprained ankle or real injury weren't making her happy, but Maggie had never been one to count on any Mounties showing up to rescue her.

As it happened, this specific Mountie had peeled out of his car and was glaring up at both of them with an exasperated scowl.

If she had her druthers, Andy would never have caught her in such a mortifying mess, but never mind that. Tarnation, he was a sight for sore eyes. She forgot the sleepless night, forgot her grumpy-bear mood, forgot all the stuff she was blaming him for. That square-boned jaw and those lethally sexy eyes plunked a sizzle in her pulse that just refused to be dislodged. Not that he was immediately looking at her.

"Colin, you let your aunt get away with this kind of thing often? I don't know how she got the confounded, crazy idea to climb up on an icy, slippery roof in the middle of winter—but couldn't you give her a whack upside the head and make her see some reason?"

Maggie swiftly elbowed her nephew in the ribs so he'd stay quiet. "Now, don't yell at Colin. Everything was going fine until I accidentally tipped over the ladder. And he thought fixing the leak was a bad idea, too. The only reason he climbed up here was because he felt compelled to help me."

"Yeah, well, I feel *compelled* to scream on both your heads." Andy bent over to right the ladder and then motioned both of them down. "Colin, you and I are going to have a little talk about the birds and the bees. Starting with when *never* to listen to a woman."

"Hey. I was going to make you hot chocolate to thank

you for being our hero, but now I'll have to rethink that offer. Your attitude's so lousy—"

"You hear this, Colin? She makes the dumb-ass move, and the guy gets blamed for having a lousy attitude. Now I ask you, would a man think with that kind of logic?"

"Um...no, sir."

"Don't you side with him," Maggie warned. But her nephew was already starting to laugh, and Andy played to it.

"We're already on the same side—trying to save you from breaking your neck. If that sun had dropped for two seconds, the difference in temperature would have made that roof a skating rink. Colin, don't you ever listen to this dimwit again—"

"Dimwit! That's *it* on the hot chocolate. Colin, don't you *ever* talk to a girl that way."

"Colin, don't you ever talk to a girl that way unless she deserves it. And in your aunt's case, if you didn't have some tender ears, I'd be reading her a serious riot act with all the language that goes with it."

As she backed down the ladder, she felt Andy's hands clamp around her hips. It was only for seconds—he was securing her balance, nothing intimate implied by his touch. But when she reached the bottom, he whirled her around, his eyes all over her like a blanket on a bed, checking for damages.

"Dammit, you're freezing to death," he muttered, and then swooped down with a spank of a kiss. She was pretty sure he meant nothing more than an impulsive gesture, expressing relief she was okay—he *had* looked a bit shaken up when he spotted her on that roof.

But as swiftly as he raised his head, his expression no longer reflected worry or relief or fury or anything like that. That short, millisecond kiss changed everything.

Their eyes connected and suddenly they were alone. Heaven knew, Colin was still right there and her nose and toes were still stinging-cold and nothing had changed in the sun-glazed snowy landscape. But Andy was somehow the only thing in Technicolor. She suddenly felt softer than a sunrise, her pulse thrumming love songs just from the way he looked at her. He touched her cheek in a gesture that seemed to say *Hi there, trouble, I missed you since yesterday.*

Colin backed down the ladder, turned around and abruptly dropped the tar bucket when he saw how they were looking at each other. "Um...listen, Mags, I really have to go home right now—"

Maggie stiffened quickly. "Nonsense, you've got to come in and get warm first. Andy, tell him."

Maggie grabbed one of Colin's arms. Andy grabbed the other. If her nephew sensed the adults were leaping on him to play chaperone, he didn't suffer from any lack of attention. Andy made hot chocolate and kept up a running lecture on handling women while Maggie changed into warm, dry cords and a bulky red sweater. By the time she came downstairs, Colin's fidgety nerves around Andy had almost disappeared—the men were chortling like goons at their own disgusting dumb-blonde jokes.

She put them to work starting a fire, charmed at Andy's subtle care and tact with her nephew. Except for a few teachers, Colin really hadn't been exposed to an adult male's influence since his dad died. She couldn't fathom why he'd responded with such initial uneasiness around Andy, but Andy's drawling, dry humor and easy ways seemed to have warmed Colin up. By the time they'd finished constructing a macho-sized blazing fire, the two really seemed to be hitting it off—at least until Andy suggested ordering a pizza.

Colin immediately lurched to his feet, his gaze darting between the two of them. "Oh, man, I don't know, I don't think you guys really need a third person hanging around—"

Oh, yeah, they did, Maggie thought. But to Colin she just said, "You almost froze your behind off because of me. I'm still feeling guilty that I got you involved in my roof leak. At least stay for a pizza, okay?"

"I don't think so. Mom'll be worried where I am. And I'm supposed to be home, doing chores—"

"Call your mom," Andy said. "She won't mind your having dinner with the sheriff, even if it means you're skipping chores. Trust me. I've got an 'in' with moms like you can't believe."

They conned him into staying for pizza, and set up a picnic on the carpet in front of the hearth, with Colin sitting between them. She didn't look at Andy. He didn't look at her. And the boys persisted with their exhausting run of women-put-down jokes until Maggie interrupted.

"My turn. How many men does it take to change a roll of toilet paper?"

Andy raised an eyebrow in Colin's direction. "Somehow I'll bet she thinks this is the equivalent of a dumb-blonde joke. But all right, all right, I'll bite, what's the answer?"

"The answer is—who'll ever know? It's never happened in the history of the universe."

Both males stared at her blankly. And then Andy thoughtfully thwacked her on the back because she was laughing to the point of choking. "That's the other sad thing about women, Colin. You have to fake knowing when their punch lines are, because they actually think their jokes are funny."

She punched both of them…and then served the last of

the pizza. That was the longest they could get Colin to stay. "I've learned a lot this evening, sir," he said to Andy—which had the two men doing that bonding goon grin again—but her nephew still popped to his feet and hustled for his jacket.

The instant Colin left, the atmosphere changed faster than lightning. Andy hauled their pizza debris to the kitchen, and since Cleopatra was begging with her paws on the glass doors, Maggie stepped outside to feed the raccoon some salad scraps. It wasn't like there was suddenly silence. It wasn't like they suddenly had nothing to *do*. But Colin's presence had been as good as having a priest in residence to guarantee no wayward thoughts would cross her mind, and suddenly there was just that warm blaze of firelight in a shadowy room and Andy.

As he ambled in from the kitchen, Maggie hunched down to feed the fire another log. "You were wonderful with Colin."

"He seemed like a great kid. Although I got the impression something was bugging him, Maggie. Not really like he had a chip on his shoulder, more like there was something worried in those eyes. You know if something's on his mind?"

Her brows arched at the question. "Actually, I could have sworn the opposite was true. He's had a rough year, but as of Thanksgiving, everything seemed to turn around for him. In fact, I was teasing my sister about his being such an angel lately."

"Well, maybe he was nervous because of me. Most teenagers tend to get a little nervous around a guy with a badge. Nothing odd about that." Andy scratched his chin. "If I remember being fifteen, I had a lot of ideas—most of them hormone-driven—and nothing I'd want a parent or the law to know. You said he'd been in trouble?"

"Mischief. Not trouble." Maggie stood up and dusted her hands. "There are just no adult men in his life right now, Andy. He's really missed his dad."

"Well, I wanted to get to know him. Mostly because he's your family and I know he's important to you, but also...well, if something comes up, maybe he'll figure he can talk to me."

"I sure hope it doesn't. My sister's so fragile now—I'm afraid she'd have a real stroke if either of the boys got in serious trouble."

Andy lifted the fireplace grate back in place. "Sometimes that's a lot to put on a kid. Everybody makes mistakes. The trick is, making sure a kid learns from 'em instead of having that mistake become who they are."

"That's an awfully wise insight for a small-town cop, Gautier."

He grinned. "I keep trying to convince you I'm a smart guy—only I don't seem to be smart enough to figure out what we're going to do now. Your nephew saved us for a while, but now what's gonna stop you from throwing yourself at me?"

She parked her fists on her hips. "Why, you dog. Accusing *me* of having dark, immoral, sinful intentions?"

"Hey, I'm the innocent one in this pair. You're the one with the secret in your past, Killer."

She hadn't forgotten her little amnesia problem; it seemed to hound her mind like a mosquito bite she couldn't quite scratch, but Andy somehow always found a way to make her smile about it. "Well, your virtue is safe for a few minutes. At least I was going to suggest a movie? But I just realized, I never asked you how long you could stay—"

"Truthfully I only meant to stop by for a few minutes, not stick through dinner or stay anywhere near this long.

But I can do a movie. Just have to skedaddle pretty fast after that. I've still got some paperwork I have to wrap up at the office, and a five o'clock start-up time tomorrow morning.''

His work schedule aside, Maggie figured he was subtly letting her know that he wasn't going to press to spend the night. She told herself she felt relieved...not frustrated. "Okay then, how about if I throw some popcorn in the microwave while you pick out one of the VCR tapes?"

While she poured homemade root beer and waited for the popcorn, he shuffled through her VCR tapes with a hammed-up appalled expression. "What is this, all horror and blood and guts?"

She laughed. "You want Bambi, rent a niece. To tell the truth, I've got a drawerful of girl movies. I just assumed you'd rather see a little more action."

"You assumed right. God, you've even got a collection of old Hitchcocks...although I'm not sure I can watch *Psycho* without you on my lap to save me during the scary parts."

"Uh-huh. Have you tried that line on women often, Gautier?"

"Actually...no." When she brought down the snack tray, Andy had already installed himself on the couch with his feet up. That wicked crooked grin of his suddenly faded. His eyes met hers as if they'd been waiting all through pizza and Colin's visit to find her again. He really wasn't handing her some accomplished flirt's line. He was making this up as he went. As was she. But all their mutual teasing about keeping their hands off each other wasn't entirely a joke.

Maggie could be in his arms in two seconds flat if he asked.

She suspected he could be in hers likewise.

But he said quietly, "Mags, you *are* safe sitting with me. I told you straight about needing to pack it in early. The Christmas season always makes for an extra workload. I really do have to leave, it's not a choice. But that does happen to mean that you couldn't be safer with a monk tonight."

His bluntness disarmed her every time. Andy just seemed to tackle everything honestly, a quality she'd never found in any other man. But in this case, such honest intentions didn't seem worth the price of beans.

She plunked next to him on the navy-blue couch, then eventually snuggled up to him—*Psycho* was a terrifying movie, after all. They scooped up handfuls of butter-dripping popcorn, both of them riveted on the screen, their stocking feet propped on the coffee table. Still, minute by minute she felt increasingly conscious of Andy. Smiles shared in the darkness had nothing to do with Hitchcock's plot. The long arm scooped around her shoulder had nothing to do with the fear-generated suspense in the flick. Her pulse picked up the edgy beat of desire. She wanted him. Enough to make her body feel stinging alive and uneasy with how powerful and insistent her pulse kept thrumming that drumbeat.

She hoped he didn't know. He didn't seem to. When the credits rolled, she punched off the VCR and Andy promptly lurched to his feet. "Nobody does it like Hitchcock. He's in a class of his own. And I'd sure rather be staying and watching another from your collection, but I really have to hit the road. Walk me to the door?"

She carried the popcorn bowl and two root beer glasses to the kitchen, while he found his boots and pulled on his alpaca jacket. Once he seemed ready to go, she walked him down the hall and reached out to flick on the light by the door.

He reached out to flick it off again...and in the sudden murky shadows, hooked her wrists and swung them around his neck. "Okay," he said sternly. "Two minutes of necking by the clock. No more. And no clothes off. Those are the rules."

She wanted to chuckle at his hammed-up stern tone, but her heart was suddenly thumping and every place their bodies touched seemed insufferably warm. "Excuse me? Who gave you the power to make the rules, Gautier? You'd better know right now, I don't take orders from nobody."

"Sheesh. You could at least see if you like the rules before you start talking mutiny."

He'd barely pounced before she discovered that she didn't like his rules. At all. Even remotely. She could taste the coming kiss even before he bent his head. By the time his lips touched down, the blood was sluicing through her veins like a rushing whirlpool.

The day she'd met him, she'd formed the instant, instinctive impression that he was a good man. Now she realized how completely she'd misread his character. The man was bad clear through.

He leaned her up against the wall as if it were a vertical mattress. Then took her mouth as if he owned it, like a man with a big greed staking a claim on his own private gold mine. Thighs rubbed against thighs. His taste, his scent, the pressure of those urgent, demanding kisses went straight to her head. Her breasts cushioned against his hard, muscular chest until they started to feel tight and hot, and still he kissed her. Drinking her in. Teasing her. Arousing her.

Holy kamoly. It wasn't like his kisses before this had

been gloves-on polite. And it wasn't like his unshakable patience and control had instantly disappeared, more like he was showing her a dark, dangerous wildness like a promise. Gentleness was a choice. Sometimes. Driving a woman stark out of her mind was another choice. Sometimes.

At this precise moment, Andy seemed intensely motivated to pursue option number two and to hell with sanity.

A dark, wet kiss turned deeper, slower…softer. She sighed a breath and came back for more. His jacket bunched between them. Her bulky red sweater turned steam-hot and sticky. So many clothes between them, yet she felt oddly shivery, as if she were a virgin overloading with anticipation and nerves and had no idea what to do with this tumultuous tidal wave of sensation.

What scared her more was that she really didn't know. Desire wasn't new. She could have sworn she felt comfortable with her hormones. But this wasn't just about body parts igniting from his specific touch. His big hands slid down her body, claiming, caressing, finally cupping her fanny to rock her tight and evocatively against him, but that was only part of the avalanche of emotions sweeping her under.

She couldn't remember tasting yearning before—not yearning gone amok, not a feeling of belonging so intense that doors creaked open inside her that had never been unlocked. This wasn't safe. This aching feeling to belong to him—with him—was rattlingly unfamiliar. She had a terrible feeling she was falling in love with him. Not a little in love, but hopelessly, soaringly, irrevocably down the tubes. And in Maggie's view, any intelligent woman backed off when she sensed she was in serious danger— and certainly didn't invite more.

Yet she was. Inviting more. Matching wild kiss for wild

kiss, rubbing back, evocatively teasing him no different than he was arousing her. She'd never once doubted her self-control before, knew darn well that she could handle her hormones. It was all Andy's fault this was different. Even when desire was tearing through her like a 747, sex and hormones seemed a paltry explanation for the emotions overwhelming her. That petrified four letter *L* word kept seeping into her heart's pulse. She wasn't *ready,* she kept telling herself, yet the damn man seemed to inspire this dreadful magical thing in her that just had no stop button...

Slowly he lifted his head. Slowly, his hands dropped from intimate territory and reached up to smooth a strand of hair from her temple. "I think our two minutes were up ten minutes ago. It's magic every time, isn't it, Mags? And getting worse instead of better."

"Andy..." She still couldn't breathe right. And darkness or no darkness, the way his eyes burned on her face made her want to shiver from the inside out. She swallowed hard. Somehow feelings between them had gone too far and become too complex to not confront where they were going. But she just didn't know how to be as honest about emotions as Andy did. "Look, I know you were joking about the rules. But you can't like being teased like this. It isn't fair, and I'm uncomfortable doing this to you."

"I'd be uncomfortable if I felt you were being rushed. And I have this feeling the whole world's gonna change once we make love."

She had the same feeling—that they were moving rocket-fast toward making love together. And instinctively, frighteningly certain that nothing in her life would be the same once they did. "I need to seriously tell you something."

"Okay."

"I don't know what you're expecting, but I'm not sure what I can promise you, Andy." She took a breath. "I don't have a great history with successful relationships. I've been in love, serious love, twice. Both times didn't work out because of me."

He raised an eyebrow. "I'll be damned. The way I always heard it, it took two to tango. This was different and it was all your fault, huh?"

He made her smile, but not for long. "Maybe it was. At the time I thought those relationships were good. That we understood each other. But maybe I'm too independent to pull my weight in a relationship, or to understand how to do it right, because they seemed to want me to be somebody I'm not. I have a real fear that I'm going to let you down."

Andy leaned back against the opposite wall, as if making sure they couldn't touch. "You think I'm suddenly going to want you to turn into a clinger?"

"Not…exactly. But I'm worried about disappointing you. It's happened before. Maybe I'm not going to make you feel needed the way a man likes to feel needed."

Andy hesitated then, too. "Need and independence are two separate things. As far as independence—I respect and admire that in you, Maggie, but I'm not sure how you'd define your need for autonomy. I thought your going up on that roof today was dangerous. If you expect me to shut up, never intrude if I think you're doing something dangerous—that won't happen. Far as I'm concerned, caring about you gives me the right to speak up."

She smiled. A natural, real one this time. "No sweat there. And I feel the same way. Your choices are your choices, but I reserve the right to yell at you if I think you're aiming towards something hurtful. And I admit, going up on the roof today was dumb."

He didn't dwell on it. "Okay. On to the 'need' question. I think likely I have the same fears you do. I had a marriage where I was overneeded. My job matters to me. I can't make a relationship work if the woman's going to sweat every time I get a call in the middle of the night. Been there, done that, and made me as miserable as it made her. If you're uncomfortable with what I do, I need to hear it from you."

"I'm not."

He eased away from the wall, started buttoning his jacket. "Seems to me that choosing to be with someone…that's a healthy kind of 'need.' But not if you're counting on someone else to solve your problems. Or expecting someone else to have answers for what makes you happy. Or for loneliness—hell, you can be just as lonely with the wrong person. Easier to live alone."

She nodded, breathing suddenly real soft. She felt exactly the same way.

"But someone to count on, Maggie. That isn't about need. That's about trust. Finding someone who'll be there when the chips are down…I don't see that as weakness. Or clinging. I see it as the golden part of loving somebody."

"Dammit, Gautier. You say things sometimes that just turn my knees to butter. I think you're doing it deliberately. You're just trying to inspire me into seducing you, aren't you?"

With a wicked grin, he leaned over and kissed the tip of her nose. "Killer?"

"What?"

"Promise me you'll hold that thought until the next time we're together."

Eight

Hold that thought indeed.

Maggie scowled at the computer monitor. She wasn't considering seducing Andy. Right now she wasn't even thinking about him—which she'd told herself at least a dozen times.

Shutters blocked out a blustery winter afternoon. Her fingers clicked on the computer keys somewhere between 110 and 120 miles an hour. Her answering machine was on. A sign at her back door threatened dire consequences to anyone who interrupted her. She was barefoot and wearing old white sweats with a hole in the fanny—her dead-serious working clothes. A cranberry candle was lit next to her, wafting its scent through her office.

A deadline was looming. Four days from now she needed to trek into Mytron in Boulder with a finished manual in hand. She'd always worked best with a panther nipping at her heels, and she knew her engineering guys like brothers. The boys were all brilliant—but they couldn't communicate worth bologna in the English language. Their technical manuals used to require a translator for a customer to comprehend their mumbo-jumbo technobabble…not to mention their dangling participles.

They needed her—which she'd certainly clearly told them. She was worth her weight in gold—which she'd also told them, but totally astounding her for years now, she'd never expected them to pay her as if they believed it.

The telephone jingled. She ignored it. Dishes were piled in her sink. Four fresh inches of snow needed a shovel. She really should get around to brushing her hair sometime today. But typically when she was on a marathon work stretch, total immersion was her modus operandi. The rest of life had permission to go hang—but it seemed there was one teensy exception today.

Andy's face kept popping into her mind. That slow, lazy grin. The dark eyes. The black lightning sizzling in the air every time he touched her. She'd paced the floor for two nights running, trying to analyze the soul connection she felt for him. He said things she'd long believed. She valued the same stuff he did. Maybe the gale force attraction had her knees knocking some—she admitted being rattled, even a little scared, at how blindly she seemed to melt around Andy. Yet being with him felt as natural and right as she'd ever felt with another human being.

It was all going good.

Too good.

Nothing was that perfect. Nothing. Everybody knew relationships took work. Everybody knew there were problems and differences to be sorted out, so damnation, where were the glitches? Why didn't they show up? Maggie knew darn well she was two inches away from diving off a cliff with him, but somewhere below there had to be a rock. There always was.

The telephone quit ringing the instant the answering machine kicked on. A telemarketer, she assumed, and kept working.

Five minutes later, the phone jangled again. She ignored it again. Three rings later the machine started its leave-a-message spiel. "Maggie? It's Joanna—if you're home, please pick up."

Maggie vaulted out of her chair and grabbed the phone. "I'm right here, hon."

"I really hate to bother you. You're probably right in the middle of working—"

"I'm not doing a thing. Don't worry about it." Her sister's voice sounded so slurry and strange that a dozen alarm bells went off in Maggie's head.

"I'm just having trouble. With the car. I'm in town. Christmas shopping again. By Mulliker's. And I just don't know what to do—"

"Take it easy. I'll be right there. Go inside where it's warm—like pop inside June's and grab a cup of coffee. I'll be there before you finish it."

Maggie grabbed her long coat—a way to cover her disgraceful sweats rather than wasting time changing clothes. Fifteen minutes later she was circling Main Street for the second time. Finally she found a parking spot three blocks from either Mulliker's or June's coffee shop. There was no help for it. With only two weeks before Christmas now, every shopper in the county seemed to be in town. She hustled out and started hiking. Swirling snow stung her eyes and nipped at her cheeks as she passed by ho-ho-ing Santas and carolers. Every doorway had jingling bells; red ribbons were even hanging from the traffic lights.

Reaching her sister was the only goal on her mind, not

the Christmas spirit right then and certainly not shopping...yet when she stopped at the crosswalk light, her gaze flashed to one of the storefront windows at Mulliker's. A guy's leather jacket was being showcased.

She just accidentally glanced at it. As jackets went, the style looked both pricey and more a teenager's definition of ultracool than anything that would appeal to her—there was nothing particularly outstanding about it. Certainly no reason in the universe to explain why her stomach suddenly clenched and her freezing hands suddenly felt slippery-damp inside her gloves.

It was just a jacket. Nothing to her. No one she knew wore anything like it. Yet adrenaline seem to pump through her veins in a gushing rush, overwhelming her with feelings of guilt and anxiety. For a few seconds she had the mortifying feeling that she was going to be sick— but then the traffic light changed. Impatient shoppers jostled behind her; one woman shot her a dirty look for standing in the way.

Maggie quickly moved, and forced her attention on getting to her sister and nothing else, but she still felt totally exasperated with herself. Enough was enough. Her mini-amnesia problem was annoying enough, but these chronic and unfathomable guilt attacks had simply gone too far.

She'd always prided herself on her strength, had never copped out from facing a problem before. It was past time she figured out what the patooties was causing this anxiety and handled it, for Pete's sake.

As faces blurred past her, she thought of Andy again— specifically of his deadpan expression when he called her "Killer." He got such a charge out of teasing her about her wild, criminal ways. He always made her laugh, made her feel better...yet still she considered whether her relationship with Andy might not be tailgating her lost-memory problem.

Obviously he had nothing to do with the day of the accident; she hadn't even known him. But this pervasive, invasive instinct that she'd done something wrong was still haunting her. Andy joked every time she confessed to past mistakes. But she *had* made mistakes, big mistakes, in relationships in the past. Andy's easy acceptance of her was a balm to her woman's soul. But the magic between them, the way the relationship had developed so perfectly, increasingly worried her.

She was afraid of disappointing him. Andy's ethics and values were so strong that she feared his expectations of her were higher than she could live up to. She didn't want to let him down. He mattered so much; she'd come to care too deeply. If she failed him, it would be like failing herself. And maybe that was why the lost twenty-four hours kept bugging her. Could that feeling of guilt be some kind of warning?

You're thinking in circles, she told herself impatiently. All this analyzing was getting her nowhere, and the only immediate problem on her mind should have been her sister. She reached June's coffee shop and swiftly pushed open the door.

The place was packed, and the homey decor had a decidedly seasonal flavor. One Santa was sipping hot chocolate at the counter; another was wolfing down a piece of pecan pie. Boots dripped snow everywhere; shoppers' packages clogged the aisles, and bulky coats draped over chair backs. The smell of warm cinnamon rolls and coffee wafted through the air. Crowd or no crowd, Maggie spotted her sister in two seconds flat.

Joanna was huddled at a back table. Her blond hair was like a gold beacon, and so were the distinctly fragile, delicate bones. As Maggie barrelled past the crowded tables, she saw a mountain of packages mounded next to her sister. She also saw that Joanna's gorgeous eyes looked strangely sleepy and unfocused.

"Something went wrong with your car?"

"Um…not exactly, Mags."

Maggie sank in the next chair, her gaze riveted on her sister's face. "Well, that's a good thing, since you already know I don't have the mechanical sense of a fig. Beyond making sure you weren't cheated at Harry's garage, there wasn't gonna be much I could help you with."

"I just needed a ride home, Maggie."

"Yeah, I can see that."

"I was embarrassed to tell you the problem on the phone. But I really didn't think I could drive. And I didn't want the boys to know…"

Her sister's voice was almost musically soft and slurry. Maggie kept her voice quiet, but typically she cut to the chase. "Since when did you take up drinking in the middle of the day?"

"Since never. I swear. But this morning I woke up so nervous, and I had a whole day of things I had to get done. I just thought a glass or two would help me get…centered. And it seemed to. Only I forgot to have breakfast, and then I went out and started shopping and suddenly it seemed to hit me like a steamroller."

Maggie wanted to give her a sister a whomp upside the head, but somehow she'd never managed to get mad at Joanna and didn't now. Invariably she felt helpless, not angry. She just didn't know how to instill a little steel spine into such an unworldly dreamer. "Is your stomach upset? If you need something to eat first, we'll get that and that I'll drive you home."

"My tummy's okay. But my car—"

"Don't worry about it. I'll take care of getting your car home." How, Maggie had no immediate idea. But finding a resourceful solution to that kind of problem was a piece of cake. Her sister's eyes welled, making her feel doubly helpless to solve the problem that mattered.

"Mags, I'm *sorry*. I always seem to be doing something wrong—"

"Hey, you're taking this too seriously. What's the crime? I remember making this recipe once that called for cooking sherry. Only I kept tasting it—and I ended up so potched before it was done that it's amazing I didn't burn up the kitchen."

"You're trying to make me laugh. But you were a kid then, sis. And I'm not a kid."

"I know you're not. And if you're in the mood to dip in some wine, call me and we can get goofy together. Don't do this alone again, okay?"

"I never did before. I promise. I swear that's true. Maggie, I'd never drink in front of the boys. You know that."

Yeah, Maggie knew. Her sister had been a full-time dedicated mom until this patch of grief just seemed to suck her under. Her love for the boys hadn't changed. She just seemed so lost. "Look, there's no reason to make a mountain out of a one-shot goof. You know anybody who doesn't do stupid things sometimes?"

"You don't," her sister said bleakly.

"Joanna! Of course I do! Now come on, let's see how you do standing up. I'll carry the packages. We'll get you home. And you can tell the boys their Aunt Mags is having them over for a solid junk-food dinner, get them out of your hair—"

"You're always rescuing me."

Of course she was. What was family for? Yet as she bustled Joanna out of the restaurant, one of Andy's com-

ments came back to haunt her. Maybe he was right, that
some people just never dared to get up and walk if there
was always someone around to carry them. But Andy
worked with criminals. This was her sis. What choice
could she possibly make but to be there for her sister?

Every muscle in Andy's back and neck was knotted. It
had just been one of those days. Two in the morning, the
Baileys had gotten into a brouhaha again. Mary Lee went
after Ed this time with a cast-iron skillet, but typically
once Andy showed up, Ed had remembered his macho
pride and refused to press charges. A safety program at
the elementary school had chewed up the whole morning,
and the afternoon had been nonstop. Someone spotted
Griff Windsor wandering down the highway in his shirt-
sleeves; Griff went loco at least once a year, but a town
this small couldn't support a psychiatrist, and someone
like Griff fell between the cracks. Three shoplifters before
dinner, and then an ugly three-car pileup on U.S. 70—
took him and the state cops and firetrucks, as well, before
the mess was cleared up.

He should be home. Sleeping. He knew damn well he
was crankier than a snapping turtle when he didn't get his
quota of zzz's.

Still, his hands slugged in his pockets, his boots crunch-
ing on snow, he kept walking. The town closed up at nine.
It was past eleven now, the stores long locked up, the
streets emptied of cars.

It was his town, this time of day. The mean wind that
bittered the whole day had long died, a full white moon
shining on Christmas lights and steepled roofs and the
silent, snowy streets. There was no reason to patrol; John
had the night shift covered. But the silence, the fresh sharp
air burning his lungs, seeing the yellow lamplights glow-

ing in front windows, just seemed to soothe the day's stresses. He could feel the tight muscles unknotting with every loose-limbed stride.

He turned the corner and stopped. Maggie's new white vehicle was the only car in sight. He heard sounds from behind it—metal scraping against metal, then a throaty feminine voice swearing in exasperation.

Her fanny showed up in his vision. Just her fanny, actually, appearing from behind the vehicle's rear end. Since Andy had become a recent expert in the way she filled out a pair of jeans, it wasn't like he'd mistake that particularly delectable body part for any other woman's. And then she suddenly straightened up so he could catch her whole profile—the moonlight illuminated an exasperated scowl and the dead-stubborn set of her jaw. The bell echo of another "damn" whistled through the crystalline air, then she bent back down again.

Nobody could rouse Andy's sense of humor when he was this crabby-beat. Except, it seemed, her. He had to stride closer to get a better picture. Apparently she was trying to hook a trailer to the back of her vehicle. A snowmobile—obviously intended to be towed on the mini-trailer—sat just beyond. Likely in daylight she could have managed the hookup job, but trying to do anything like that in the moonlit shadows was an uphill challenge. It wasn't hard to see she was in trouble.

She was so engrossed she obviously didn't hear him approaching. "Hey, Killer. You setting up a second getaway vehicle for your next bank robbery?"

She bolted upright with a distinctly feminine screech and a hand slapped on her heart. She looked less startled-scared than downright guilty—but that expression faded fast. The warm light in her eyes seemed to be just for him, even if she did prop two fists on her hips again. "I didn't have time to rob any banks today, but darn you, Gautier, I should have known it'd be you who'd catch me breaking the law.''

"That's the repercussion I've been trying to explain to you criminal types for some time. Sooner or later you always get caught. Only, um, I'm not exactly sure what crime you think you're committing here.''

"Well, I'm not. At this specific instant. But I drove the snowmachine through town. I know that's illegal. The thing is…I had to drive my sister home in her car, which meant I had to leave mine, which meant I had to figure out some way to pick up my car. So I waited until the town closed down, and then just kind of hoped the sound of the snowmobile wouldn't bother anybody this late. Then all I had to do was hitch up the snowmachine to my car and everything was supposed to be solved.''

"That story sounds so convoluted that I can hardly follow. Your sister got in some kind of trouble involving transportation. You helped her out. Is that about the gist?'' Andy hunkered down. Light or no light, he'd hitched up enough trailers to do it blindfolded—and waiting for Maggie to ask for help wouldn't likely pay off in this millennium. Having seen the sisters in action before, Andy figured he didn't need more of the story to figure that out either. Maggie seemed to play a regular white knight-ess for her sister. Whether Maggie got stuck holding a bag of problems didn't seem to get noticed by either her or Joanna.

"That's the general gist. Except for that part about knowing that nobody's supposed to drive a snowmobile in town. It's okay to give me a ticket.''

Once the minitrailer was hooked up, he and Maggie got on opposite sides of the snowmobile and rolled it up. "Well, around the Christmas season, I try to turn a blind eye to certain infractions. It'd be different if I thought you could be reformed. But the way you confessed, asked outright for a ticket..." Andy shook his head sadly. "Hell, I just don't think there's a lot of reform hope for a hard-core criminal mind like yours."

Her grin had more devilment than the moonlight. Still, as she strapped the machine to secure it, she said, "Now, Andy, I don't want you thinking I'd claim having pull with the law. I knew I was in the wrong, that I was risking a ticket. It's okay. I don't ever expect you to make any exceptions for me."

"I do believe I could survive the public backlash of criticism in this situation. And as it happens, Killer, you *do* have pull with the local law. If you'd just do something worth a handcuffing offense, I guarantee I'd get tough with you."

"Uh-huh. I've heard that kinky promise from you before, Gautier. You better watch it, or I might have to take up some real murder and mayhem just to see you deliver." She strode around the snowmobile, lifted up on tiptoe, and kissed him. Her lips were ice cold, the smack obviously intended to be swift. Yet her gloved hands lingered on his shoulders. And the fast smack somehow lasted long enough to heat his blood to a slow, hot-swirling simmer—and God knew the temperatures that night were subzero.

"It occurs to me you're already an expert at causing mayhem. You don't need any more experience. Was that kiss for any particular reason?"

"Love. Mad passion. And maybe a thank-you for helping me hitch up that damn thing. Although I *hate* it when men can do things better than I can."

"I'll try to remember not to help you again. Scout's honor. And speaking of bribery—"

"Beg your pardon? How did bribery get in this conversation?"

"You broke the law. Did you think I'd let you off just because I'm crazy about you? You're going to have to bribe me with something...I was thinking Christmas trees."

She went still real suddenly when he admitted being crazy about her. Her cheeks and nose were already cherry-red from cold, yet he could have sworn he saw a soft flush color her skin beyond that. Still, she chuckled and peered into his eyes as if unsure anybody sane were home in there. "You're looking tired, Andy. Adorable, but tired. You obviously had a rough day and it's late. But I'm having real trouble figuring out how you got from bribes to Christmas trees—"

"Do you usually put up a tree?"

"Actually, no...not since my parents died." She leaned against her car. So did he. "Joanna does, because she has the kids. And we usually decorate her whole place together...but I don't know. Just living by myself, I could never see going through the trouble. I put out some candles and wreaths and stuff, but that's about it."

"Same here. Once I got a divorce, there was just me. No point putting a tree up just to stare at it and remind myself I was alone. But I'm thinking...I'd like a tree this year. If I could con you into cutting one down with me. Doing it solo wouldn't be any fun."

"I could probably be conned," Maggie said wryly. She absently glanced down, as if surprised to discover her gloved fingers were twined with his gloved fingers.

He wasn't. Holding hands with her on a silent, moonlit street seemed as natural as breathing, and breathing seemed as natural as the avalanche of desire that sucked them under on other times. And that was the thing. He wanted the tree because the season was different for him this year. The difference was Maggie being part of his life.

He usually thought of Christmas as being for families, kids sneaking under the tree to peek at packages and that kind of thing. Eventually he'd like to bring up the subject of kids with her, but not yet. For now he was only thinking of a family of two. Her. Him. Starting the rituals that glued a couple together by making memories.

"Saturday morning sound okay for the tree thing?"

"Sure, sounds fine." She lifted a sudden humorous smile at him. "You realize it's almost midnight, and we're standing here in this freezing weather holding hands?"

"Pretty damn goofy."

"I'd call it sanity-challenged." But she didn't lift her hand from his clasp or make a move toward her car keys. And since she seemed in no hustle to leave him, Andy thought they might as well get some personal tricky matters out in the air.

"Do you happen to be a churchgoer, Mags?"

"Now where'd that come from? Talking religion can get a little touchy," she said carefully.

"Yeah. That was the idea. There's no way I can guess how you feel on dicey subjects like that unless you say."

She nodded, and although she kept her tone light, her eyes met his honestly. "Well...growing up, I was a pretty wild heathen, and I certainly planned on staying that way—you know how fond I am of sin and crime—and besides that, I could never seem to match my personal beliefs with any organized church. But then I moved here when Joanna's husband got cancer. And Reverend Gustofson was so good to us. He's really a dreadfully sneaky man. I'm not sure how it happened, but somehow I find myself there most Sundays."

"He *is* a good guy," Andy agreed.

"Yeah, well it's your turn in the hot seat now. You have some strong religious feelings in one direction or another?"

"Strong religious feelings, yeah. Strong feelings about churches...not exactly. I was raised believing spiritual feelings were a private thing. You go to the woods and meditate, pray your own way. My dad used to say that no church or anything else could force you to ask yourself the hard questions about right and wrong and what you believe. It has to come from the inside. But..."

"But?" she prodded him.

"But I seem to end up in one church or another on most Sundays. I know all the local reverends and priests because my job crosses paths with them. You get a troubled kid, it works to line up all forces that could be influencing his life. I can't say I'm a belonger, but my comfort level inside a church is more than it used to be. You have any problem with that?"

"No, not at all," she said quietly, and then hesitated. "Were you bringing up the religious questions for any special reason?"

"Not exactly. Just seems to me that a couple tends to get in trouble when they hide how they feel about certain kinds of things. I don't think two people ever believe exactly the same thing. Don't think they have to. But what have you got if you can't talk about the stuff that really matters to you down deep?"

"You're getting awfully serious on me, Gautier."

"Well...I might have given you the impression before that sex is the only thing on my mind. And it is, it is— ninety per cent of the time. But I thought maybe I could impress you about my being a good guy if I brought up a serious thought now and then."

"Andy?" She turned to face him. "You *are* a good guy."

Well, hell. He got a kiss that knocked his socks off without half trying. And then he bundled Maggie off before she caught her death of cold, but he stood there on the snowy street until her car lights were out of sight.

She was right about him turning serious on her. Serious enough to bring up a private, awkward subject like religion on a night that threatened frostbite. Serious enough to realize he was dead-beat-tired, mean-tired, and yet being with her made him forget every damn thing that'd gone wrong with the day.

Serious enough to realize he was drowning deep in love with her.

His heart was increasingly hanging out naked and exposed for her. She was so damned perfect for him that he wanted to kick himself just to make sure he felt the pain. Magic like this was so rare he was still scared to believe it.

And even more scared that he was risking his heart if Maggie didn't feel the same.

Nine

"I'm telling you, it'll fit."

"Maybe in the White House. You've got twelve-foot ceilings in your place?"

"Aw, come on. The tree isn't that tall."

"Andy! Stand next to it, for Pete's sake! They always look little when they're out in the woods. This sucker's a monster!"

"Height is just a detail. The thing that matters is shape, and this one's perfectly symmetrical."

Maggie threw up her hands and addressed her comments to the seamless blue sky—since getting through to Andy was a waste of energy. "You can lead a horse to water, so how come you can't do it to a man? When they've got that macho gene thing switched on, nothing seems to get through. If just one of them could reason things out like a woman…" A handful of fluffy snow landed on her shoulder—a fairly amazing feat, considering there wasn't even a lick of wind on this pricelessly sunny afternoon. She whirled around. "Did you just hit me, Gautier?"

"Offhand, I'd say 'hit' was a mighty exaggeration." Andy, standing four feet from her, had scooped up another handful of snow and was packing it tight between his gloves. "If you want to see a hit, now—"

She got him with a snowball first, right in the tummy. And managed to swivel a hip to avoid his next pitch. Then, though, she caught the look in his eyes and decided that courage was an overrated value. She turned tail and ran. "I'm warning you—if you even come near me with another snowball, I'll press charges!"

"*What* charges?"

"Darned if I know. You're the law. Can't you come up with something?"

He came up with the extremely unchivalrous idea of tackling her behind the knees. Down she went in a mountain of snow. By the time she'd recovered her stocking cap and wiped the snow off her face, she'd managed to almost quit laughing and turn around. Her eyes narrowed. "You think you're playing with some cream puff little sissy here? You're gonna pay for that, big guy."

He was so impressed with this threat that he yawned.

She couldn't conceivably let him get away with that. By any woman's standards, that yawn was justifiable motivation for retaliation without mercy. And she had that righteous intention...but for about ten seconds, she couldn't seem to move. For just that moment in time, Andy was silhouetted against a clean blue sky with a backdrop of snowy woods. His ski jacket and gloves were as snow-crusted as hers, his dark hair glistening with it, his face ruddy and his dark eyes dancing with the devil.

A feeling of love for him came at her like a tidal wave, sucking her into it, warming all the corners that had been cold for so long, making her bones feel like liquid and her heart softer than a sunlit rainbow.

Maggie had the sudden sneaky, scary feeling that recovery from this was never going to happen. It had gone too far. He'd gone too far. He'd somehow become part of her life, part of her heartbeat, part of how she defined love.

Temporarily, though, a woman had to do what a woman had to do. She climbed to her feet with two fistfuls of snow and gave chase.

Their tree outing had been supposed to take a couple hours in the morning. By the time they'd hauled the twelve-foot monster tree to his house, they'd played so many hours that it was late afternoon. They were both freezing, starved, and whipped. Andy hauled the tree through his front door, took one look at his living room, and said, "Aw hell, it's not going to fit."

Maggie chortled laughter. "If I weren't a lady, I'd say I told you so." She paused long enough to give that a second think. "Actually, I just remembered. I never once aspired to being a lady—"

"Just stop right there while you're ahead, Killer. I might even feed you—if you stick to your story about never wanting to be a lady and just forget about the tree."

She quit teasing—only because Andy was going to be stuck soon enough with the tree problem—and both of them needed a break and a chance to warm up. Andy produced four-inch double-decker sandwiches and mugs of steaming cider. She still had her hands wrapped around the warm mug as he showed her around.

Maggie had wondered where and how he lived. The

house itself was about a two-mile hike from the town center, just off in a nest of hills where he had some privacy. The location seemed a natural choice for Andy, yet it was the inside that revealed all kinds of interesting secrets about him.

They'd started in the kitchen—which needed a coat of paint, in her view, preferably any color but pea green. But he'd built in a pantry with a space for a double freezer. A brand-new microwave shared space next to a really ancient stove. The pine board table was located to get a shower of morning sun and a view of the blue spruces and golden aspens in his rambling-long backyard.

Andy's style was no frills, but everything was comfortable and practical both. The downstairs bathroom was white-tiled and spare, but the towels were crimson, huge and thirsty-thick. An extra bedroom on the main floor was tiny, with clean, Shaker-style furniture and an Indian quilt in golds and blacks draping the bed.

Andy kept checking her face for reactions. "I warned you the place wasn't fancy," he said uneasily.

"You should have warned me there'd be no dust. Now I'm ashamed that I showed you all my messes. Is this where you lived when you were married?"

"No. My ex...well, she was more into having a showpiece house. A setup for entertaining, that sort of thing. I had savings going into the marriage, but the house we had ate that up pretty quick. I never needed that kind of space just for me. Never felt like that place was mine either. This house..."

When he hesitated, she filled in. "This house has good karma."

"Well, I don't know about 'karma'," he said dryly.

"I do. For sure it's got a bachelor stamp, but it's still

a home instead of just a house. That's the difference. You walk in and it just *feels* friendly, welcoming. I really love it.'' He didn't often reveal scars from his first marriage, but Maggie easily intuited that the ''showpiece'' decorating his ex-wife valued hadn't been a home at all. Not for him. ''Lead on, MacDuff, and show me the upstairs.''

She trailed him up the narrow staircase, where there was another bathroom, a long, low cedar-paneled den slanted under the eaves and a giant master bedroom. In typical man fashion, Andy was just popping her in and out of rooms so she could see the place, not really giving her time to linger and study. Still, she found herself stalled in the bedroom doorway.

She didn't mean to, but Andy's austere style was even more pronounced here. There was no clutter—no shoes, no clothes strewn around. Even his loose change was neatly contained in a tray on the dresser. The walls were painted a pale gray, which at least didn't clash with the chocolate down comforter on the king-size bed.

Her gaze pounced to the bed—partly because she could too easily imagine his sleeping alone and lonely on that huge expanse of mattress...partly because she could too easily imagine waking up wrapped up in that chocolate down comforter next to him. Thankfully there was something hanging from the bedpost to distract her attention from those wayward thoughts. She recognized the item as a dream catcher—the only frill of any kind she'd spotted in the whole house.

''Does it work?'' she murmured. ''Does it trap your dreams so they're not lost?''

''You'd have to sleep here to find out. In fact, if you want to audition the bed to see how it works—''

She turned, to find that familiar wicked glint in his

eyes. He'd teased her before. She couldn't fail to give back as good as she got. "Listen, buster—you invite amoral, immoral criminal types in your bed, you risk all kinds of repercussions," she said severely.

"That was especially the part I was looking forward to."

Darn it, Maggie could feel her pulse galloping and an embarrassing flush climbing her cheeks. She'd sensed, when he invited her to his place, that Andy could have something in mind for the end of the evening. She also recalled how many times he'd teased her before—verbally and physically—and then abruptly turned into a gentleman on her. Judging from her racing pulse, her heart seemed to be considering whether she'd let him get away with that gentleman routine if he tried pulling it on her tonight.

Her heart was all big talk. Being sure she could deliver on the action wasn't so easy. And Maggie knew he meant another teasing comment right then, but somehow her voice turned low and serious. "Andy...you could be really disappointed, you know."

"Mags?"

"What?"

"It'll freeze in the desert before I could conceivably be disappointed in you, or anything about you. Now, for Pete's sake, try and get your mind off sex for ten minutes, woman. We have a Christmas tree to put up."

Of course he had to trim three feet off the tree and shave down the trunk. The job—no surprise—erased any further sexual innuendos from his mind and involved a great deal of swearing. All the years Maggie was growing up, she'd heard her dad use precisely the same language when he did his Warrior Thing with Christmas trees. The lush scent of fresh pine invaded the house.

Snow and needles and stray branches tracked in everywhere.

The tree—eventually—got located in his living room by the bay window, which left two chairs with no place to go. Since darkness had already fallen, Maggie switched on lamps and started rearranging furniture. She'd glanced around when they first walked in, but now she really had a chance to study his main living area.

The walls were paneled with rough pine. A working woodstove sat in the corner on a brick hearth. The couch and chairs were the color of bark, a quiet woodsy hue, with an Indian woven carpet picking up golds and green and more bark colors. Built-in bookshelves had a stash of tomes on Indian medicine and lore and mysticism. He'd obviously made the coffee table, and the glass top displayed an arrowhead collection—not just points but scrapers and flint knives, with two peace pipes arranged in the center.

"The pipes look really old," she commented.

"They are. I asked a museum guy to check out the collection a while back. He said the clay one's a good thousand years old—a real treasure. They were passed down from my great-gram's side of the family."

"One of the arrowhead points looks like obsidian?"

"Yeah, that's one of the fancier pieces. Native Americans didn't use money to barter back then. They used things of value. An obsidian arrowhead was considered a bride price."

"Well, hell. I'd pay it for the right guy—it's gorgeous. Tarnation, how come men were never for sale? Why did it always have to be the women?"

"Because we're smarter and bigger and stronger?"

She threatened dire retribution for that macho heresy, but just then was too busy to deliver on that threat. There was still more in the room to explore. A tall, glassed-in cabinet held a collection of guns, and when Andy caught her looking inside, he started naming them. "The long sucker is a .64 caliber Hall Harper's Ferry breech loading percussion carbine. Hanging high there is a .44 caliber Remington-Beals revolver, and beneath that a 5/Root model 1855 sidehammer Colt pistol—"

The numbers and models meant nothing to her, but his tone of voice communicated how much they meant to him. "These are all antiques, Andy?"

"Yeah. Date from the Civil War, and again passed down in the family. Today's guns are pretty obviously symbols of violence. But I dunno, these always touched me as a different kind of symbol—not about remembering things worth dying for, but about the things worth living for. Pretty corny, huh?"

"Hey, since when are values corny? I've got symbolic keepsakes, too, like my great-gram's china. Just nothing quite like your gun collection...although, actually, I do own a gun."

"You do?" Andy was hunched down by the tree, but now he turned to face her.

"Yup. Not for burglars, nothing like that. In fact, it's locked and padlocked in my attic crawl space. I honestly don't see myself capable of turning a gun on another human being, no matter what I was threatened with or what the circumstances were."

"There's that criminal mentality of yours showing up again, Killer. So what's the gun for?"

"Well...right after I moved here, a deer was hit on the road. She crawled into the ravine behind my house to die, but it wasn't happening that fast, and she was suffering terribly. I called a vet, but Doc Henley had his hands full, couldn't come out any sooner than really late

that night. It wasn't right. Letting her suffer like that.
But I didn't have anything around to help put her out of
her misery—except like a kitchen knife—and I know it
sounds cowardly, but I just couldn't make myself use it.
I just couldn't—''

''Maggie, quit thinking so guilty. You've got plenty
of courage. That's just a really hard thing to do, for anybody.''

She felt an instant warm fuzzy at how swiftly Andy
defended her, but a little embarrassed that he might have
thought she was asking for it. ''Well, anyway. That's
why I bought a gun the next day, and learned how to
use it. And I think the fates must have been looking out
for me, because that's the last time I ran across a critter
in that bad a shape. All the wounded animals I've come
across have just needed a little rescuing,'' she said
lightly.

Andy responded with equal lightness. ''You rescue
critters. You rescue your sister. I don't suppose I could
talk you into rescuing me right about now?''

''Huh?''

Andy sighed. Long and heavily. ''Aw man, I've really
goofed this up. I was so hot to do this tree with you.
Only I *had* to pick a tree it'd take me two hours to cut
down to size. And I thought I was brilliantly planning
ahead by buying six or seven strands of lights—only now
I realize, I forgot to buy ornaments. My ex-wife got all
that kind of stuff with the divorce. And I knew that, for
Pete's sake, but somehow it never crossed my mind that
I don't have a single thing to decorate the tree with.''

Maggie took one look at his face and crossed the room
to hunch down next to him. From his impatient scowl it
wasn't hard to see that he was exasperated with himself.
Really exasperated. She couldn't smile—it wasn't funny

to him—but Andy was normally such a brick that it was almost a relief to discover he could suffer a moody case of the grumps just like everyone else. "You know what, Gautier?"

"What?"

"Personally," she said gravely, "I never thought a tree needed tinsel and doodads to do it right. I mean, I think lights help show it off, but why do we cover up the real thing that's beautiful, which is the tree itself? So I think it's a stroke of brilliance that you forgot the ornaments."

He rolled his eyes, but the grumpy scowl had already started fading. "You're just trying to get me to seduce you by being nice and understanding, aren't you?"

She rolled her eyes right back. "Normally I'd own up to having ulterior criminal motives, but sheesh, Gautier. I don't have to be nice to get *that* result."

"You think I'm easy?" Andy sounded wounded.

"Oh, no, you don't. We're not going down that road. If you don't quit teasing me, we're never going to finish this tree!"

He weaved the first set of lights. She threaded in the next set. When all seven strands had been roped around the tree, she insisted they turn off the living room lamps so they could ooh and aah.

"Ooh and aah?" Andy said doubtfully.

"Where were you raised, boy? The oohing and aahing is part of the ritual of Christmas tree decorating, for Pete's sake."

Well, damn. Maggie was just playing around to make him smile. She knew he was tired. She was, too. They'd not only spent hours romping in the woods, neither of them had quit hustling since they'd come back in. But once Andy switched off the lamps and came to stand beside her, silence fell between them.

Maggie looked at the tree and suddenly swallowed. Every holiday, she bought heaps of presents for her nephews, did the church thing, baked up goodies for Christmas dinner at Joanna's house. She went through the motions, but she'd blocked out any heart sentiment for the holiday since her parents died. Her mom and dad...they'd just woven so much love into Christmas that allowing those childhood memories loose only made her grief feel fresh all over again. Her dad sneaking surprises under the tree, the crèche she'd played with for hours, her mom singing carols at the top of her lungs around the house, always in a creaky soprano.... Dammit, it just hurt too much to remember. So she braced herself for the loneliness of the holidays and put on a smile and accepted that was how it was going to be for her.

But there was something about Andy's tree. Something dangerous. Something magical. The childhood memories touched down in her mind, but invoked only lightness in her heart instead of sadness. The lush scent of pine and the spirit of giving and the fat, soft branches mounded with star-like lights and the hush in the room...

When Andy's hand suddenly touched hers, she turned, her arms lifting to wind around his neck. She anticipated his kissing her, and she wanted that kiss. Needed it. Welcomed it.

Yet he folded her up in a quiet, warm bear hug and just held her. Heartbeat to heartbeat, cheek to cheek. Maggie was so used to sexual chemistry combusting between them that the simple, snuggling hug seemed to tear at something inside her. Maybe she'd known she was falling in love with him, but these sensations were all new. Andy felt like…family. Not just lover, but mate. The silly, ordinary old Christmas tree felt uniquely theirs, a bond between them. And that sweet, consuming feeling of love kept coming.

She lifted her head, and his eyes were waiting for her. Thinking of a man as "family" was hardly an erotic thought, yet when he bent down, his lips brushed hers like the whispery stroke of a feather, and suddenly the lustful, earthy sensations Andy invoked in her were all there, too. The richness of loving him seemed to add fresh clarity to her hearing, new colors her eyes had never noticed before, electric intensity in every texture and taste.

One soft kiss chained into another, then another. His whiskery chin nuzzled her neck. His hands moved slower than honey, kneading a trail of sensation down her spine and ribs, wooing her closer, molding her closer. She tasted tenderness in the soft, dark sweep of his tongue. She tasted wonder. She tasted the loneliness he brought her, the honesty of naked emotion he'd always revealed to her, and felt something huge and scared and overwhelming well up in her heart.

"I think you must be really hot in that sweater," he murmured.

"Miserably hot," she murmured back. "Andy?"

He didn't immediately answer, while he was unraveling the sweater over her head. And once her face showed up again, he seemed compelled to kiss her before answering her either. "What?"

"This is a crazy moment to tell you this. But I just want you to know. My parents would have loved you." She reached for the buttons on his shirt.

"I already suspected I would have liked them. I only have to look at the daughter they raised. But I think you've got that a little wrong, Killer. Your dad would probably have brought out his shotgun if he knew what I had in mind for his daughter."

"Well. Possibly. And dads are just touchy that way, they can't help it. But my dad...he always knew a good man when he found one." She peeled the flannel shirt from his shoulders, paused to kiss the hollow in his throat. "Um, Andy?"

"You thought of another touchy thing you wanted to bring up around right now?"

"It's a short question," she assured him. "I've just been getting this feeling... You're not gonna pull that honorable, gentleman thing on me tonight, are you?"

"Nope. I have in mind...getting as naked with you as two people can get. Making love with you all through the night and into the morning. Right here. Upstairs. Couch, floor, bed, kitchen table. Anything that suits your fancy. But you happen to have a major vote in this, Killer. You can add or subtract anything on that agenda at any time—"

She didn't mean to cut him off, but his rough, low voice was sending shivers down her spine. Instinctively she pulled his head down to hers, answering him physically instead of verbally.

And he answered back, with a kiss so volatile that her knees felt shaky. His bare chest looked bronzed in the tree light, tufts of scratchy hair tickling her own bare skin. He pushed down her bra straps, trapping her arms, glazing kisses down her collarbone and the slope of her shoulder. By the time he'd eased her down to the carpet, her bra had disappeared and the snap of her jeans had been thumbed open.

She unsnapped his, saw his eyes fire like wet black ebony before he ducked his head. He roughed the tips of her breasts with his tongue, laved the undersides, the hollow over her heart…until she twisted on top and leveled him with a hot, wet kiss of her own. Her hands rushed over his shoulders, chest, learning him, hurrying, the playground of his body new to her, the freedom to touch him igniting a feeling of urgency.

"Easy," he whispered.

But she suddenly couldn't do easy. Danger was clamoring through her pulse. Andy looked strong and pagan and huge in the soft light. Not frightening. But…she'd known this moment was coming. Both were too old to keep teasing each other. She wanted this, wanted him, wanted and knew they were both ready to take the relationship to deeper, darker waters. Andy wasn't one to play with a woman. She wasn't playing with his feelings either.

She slipped her hand down his ribs to the open V of his jeans. Her teeth took a nip from his shoulder. Her hands kneaded, molded, claimed like a woman very sure of her man, a woman who wanted her man to know exactly what he was doing to her, a woman not afraid to be honest and bold—not with her lover. Not with Andy. She wanted this, wanted to make love with him beyond all reason, beyond anything she could remember. It just had to be fast, that's all. Because her pulse was rattling like a fragile leaf in a high wind. Because she was furious at those rattling nerves and she was positive they'd go away if she just…

"Maggie?"

No talk. She didn't want talk. She claimed his mouth in a pressure-cooker kiss, her eyes closed against the twinkling lights. She tried to concentrate on him. On his slick, warm skin. On the feel of his thick hair ruffling through her fingers. On the anticipation of his taking her.

"Mags. Stop." His voice came out rusty and rough. But his hands suddenly framed her face, holding her still for that instant so he could study her eyes, her expression. "Something's wrong. Tell me."

"Nothing's wrong. Nothing. I promise. I want you, Andy—"

"I thought you did." The austere set of his jaw spoke to how hard he was fighting for control. "But then your hands started trembling and you're suddenly racing like a dragon's chasing your tail. I happen to like roller-coaster speeds. Fast, slow—it's all good to me. I figure if we don't get it right the first time, we can practice for a couple hundred years. But I never figured on you being afraid."

"I'm not afraid."

"Not of anything I ever noticed before now," he murmured humorously. Or almost humorously. His shoulders were still stiff with tension. "If you're not sure of this, it's not going to work out for either of us."

"I'm sure. It's just..."

When she hesitated, he said, "No, don't clam up on me. Just blurt it out. Get it said."

She swallowed hard. "It's about...the accident I had. The dreams. You know how you tease me by calling me Killer? And I know you don't believe I could possibly have a big immoral, criminal past."

"You've got that right."

"And I like your teasing, Andy." She had to swallow again. "It's just that those dreams haven't gone away, and neither has that horrible feeling of guilt. The thing is, I don't know why or how I could have such a feeling unless it were based on something I'd seriously done. And when I realized we were going to make love, I got scared...that maybe I did something so bad that you couldn't accept it. Something that would change your feelings about me. Something that you had a right to know before our relationship went this far."

He was silent for a long moment. And then he shifted away from her, sat up, and reached for his shirt. Feeling miserably awkward, she grabbed for clothes then, too, and yanked on her sweater. The twinkling lights of the tree no longer seemed soft and magical, but harsh in her eyes. When he still said nothing, she crouched up on her knees.

"I've made you angry?" she asked.

"Not angry." He hesitated. "Yeah. Angry. I know how bugged you've been about not being able to remember those twenty-four hours. But I also know damn well you never committed a crime or did anything wrong, Maggie. So do you. I know your values by now. I know your ethics, for Pete's sake."

"Andy, you're not listening—that's the problem. That you think I'm too good—"

"Hell, yes, I think you're good. And one of the most honest people I know, but not about this. If you weren't willing or ready to make love, all you had to do was say so. Not trump up an excuse. I thought we were building something. That we both wanted the same thing…look, let's just get dressed. I'll drive you home."

They both pulled on jeans, and then winter jackets and boots in silence. Maggie didn't want to leave it like that, but she didn't know what to say. She'd ruined the mood, and knew that, but she had no idea how to make Andy understand. However foolish it sounded to him, the dreams and anxiety attacks had been dead real for her. And the deeper her relationship had gotten with Andy— the more she understood his sense of honor and integrity—the more those guilt attacks preyed on her mind.

His teasing had once reassured her, but now only added to her worry that he didn't seem to believe she could do anything wrong.

He didn't know her, if that were true. And making love had just seemed a huge land mine, if he'd built up expectations about her that she couldn't possibly meet.

Biting cold slammed them both in the teeth when they walked outside. His car was frigid, almost as frigid as his stone expression. The drive to her place only took ten minutes, not enough time for the car to warm up, but ample time for her to realize that Andy's unyielding silence wasn't coming from meanness or even anger.

She'd hurt him. Badly.

He obviously believed she'd trumped up an excuse not to make love with him. And what kept stabbing her heart was understanding how he'd come to that conclusion. That's what it had to look like, to him. When she mentally replayed her bungling part in that conversation, that's what it sounded like, even to her.

He braked in her drive, climbed out of the car, clipped the door closed. "I'll walk you in."

"You don't have to."

"Maggie, you're not walking into a pitch-black house in the middle of the night when you're with me. That's that. Now give me your key."

"I know you're mad—"

"Yeah, well, I'm mad in a way I'll get over. I love you, Killer. And I'm in love with you. Just because I happen to be royally ticked at you at the moment doesn't mean we won't get past this. Right now, if I try talking, all I'm gonna do is growl at you. Forget it—just give me your key and let's get you inside and then we'll just call this whole night off. Start over fresh tomorrow."

She heard him. He *was* growling. Conceivably close

to tearing a serious strip off her, judging from the intimidating hunch of his shoulders and the black fire in his eyes. Any female over the age of ten knew better than to cross a certain line when a man was in a temper. But this wasn't any man. It was *her* man, and the word came out of her mouth before she could stop it.

"No," she said.

Ten

"No?" Andy echoed. "What is that no supposed to mean? No, you're not going to give me your house key because you'd rather stand out here talking until we freeze to death? No, you don't want to start over fresh tomorrow because you're too ticked to even talk to me—?"

"I can unlock my own damn house, Gautier, so you can just quit barking at me." She charged past him and stabbed the house key into the lock, then pushed open the door hard enough to hear the slam-bang when it hit the opposite wall. "Come in here. Before we both get frostbite."

"Mags." Andy heaved a sigh and struggled for patience. "This is dumb. We're both mad. And both getting testier by the minute. Let's just write this off as not our night, okay? Go in, get a good night's sleep, then we'll talk tomorrow. I'm never for running from a problem, but we're both obviously wired—"

"Wired? You think I'm wired?"

Andy rubbed ice-cold fingers at the nape of his neck. He didn't figure it was a real safe idea to answer that question. In fact, he figured he'd have better luck handling a truckload of plastic explosives than Maggie at the moment.

His stomach was churning nerves. Somehow he'd managed to blow the whole day. Chewed up the morning playing with her in the snow instead of getting the tree done and up. Then he got a tree too big. Then he forgot the ornaments. And then his big plan—about trying a nice, soft, low-key, don't-scare-her seduction in front of their first tree together—well, that couldn't have gone worse. He knew damn well Mags was too independent to ever rush into any aspect of the relationship, but he'd really thought they'd worked past those fears of hers. He'd been so positive she was willing that her sudden balking really bit.

The witch-black sky was spitting snow sharper than ice. Sexual frustration was still growling on his mood, and instead of being able to call off this nightmare day, it just seemed to be getting worse.

"I'll have you know I'm not the *least* wired," Maggie informed him furiously.

"Okay, okay, you're not wired..." His pacifying tone was a waste of breath. Leaving her door wide open, she charged back toward him in her clunky boots, with the wind spinning in her hair and her eyes shooting fire. Her hands were clenched in tight fists as if she were close to punching something—like him—and her voice had a helluva bellow for a soprano.

"You think you're alone in this, buster? I happen to be in love with you, too. Totally. So damn much I'm all shook up. But that's the way it is, so if you think you're going home tonight, you've got another think coming.''

Andy hadn't been absolutely positive she wasn't going to slug him. She'd sure looked a tad out of control. Her avowal of love couldn't have stunned him more—like the sun showing up in a blizzard. Of course, she was pretty ticked. She may not have meant it. "Um, Mags…''

"I was *never* trumping up an excuse. I was telling you the truth. I *know* you think I'm making too much of the amnesia thing and those stupid anxiety attacks. Cripes, so do I. If I could just give myself a whack upside the head and make it go away, believe me, I would—''

Aw, hell. He brushed the bangs out of her eyes, because they were all wet and dripping and besides that, he needed an excuse to touch her. But that wasn't to say he was buying her story wholesale. "Come on, Maggie. Cut it out. I don't know why you're having those bad dreams, but it just couldn't be about anything connected to the night of the accident. I don't care how much it's bugging you that you can't remember—you know yourself. You couldn't possibly have done anything that's worth all this worry. Hell, I can't imagine you kicking a puppy if a gun were held to your head.''

"Well, dammit, neither can I.'' Although admitting that didn't make her sound any happier or less aggravated. "I just can't shake the feeling that I've done something wrong—and that it could matter. To you. To us. But right now, the point isn't whether I'm imagining this dumb fear. I just need you to believe me. That it was real, that I wasn't trumping up an excuse. I *want* to make love with you!''

Maybe in twenty years, this was going to strike him as funny. He'd never imagined a woman—much less Maggie—belligerently arguing about making love with him.

Particularly in the middle of a driveway on a slashing-snow, mean-cold black night, when both of them were beat and darn near freezing to death.

Andy figured a shot of whiskey'd go down real easy around now. Damned if he knew what he was supposed to do or say. Regardless what she claimed, he believed Maggie was "in the mood" like he believed cats flew. Yet worry kept thudding through his pulse, some masculine instinct that he was wading in touchy, dangerous waters if he handled this wrong.

He took a breath. "Mags, if you're sure you want me to come in, I'll come in."

"I want you to come in. What do you think I've been yelling about?"

"And if you want me in your bed, God knows, that's where I want to be."

"I couldn't possibly have told you more honestly that's exactly what I want—"

"And then we're going to sleep."

Her mouth was wide open to agree with him again. But that comment made her pause. "Sleep?"

"Just sleep."

"Just sleep," she echoed.

"I hate to keep turning into a gentleman on you, Killer. I've been looking forward to your corrupting me for some time. But somehow it just doesn't seem right to make love when you look more ready to shoot me than kiss me. So that's my theory on this. We try getting a good night's sleep. Just sleep. And if you feel differently in the morning, we could renegotiate a different program."

"You actually think that theory's gonna work?"

"Yup." Well, that was a fib. But Andy was damn sure making love with her could turn out disastrous, unless he knew the real truth of why she'd pulled back from him earlier. And he wasn't real positive he could pull back himself if he got his arms around her again. He didn't want to leave her, though. Not for the night, not even an hour, and this was a way he didn't have to. "Of course making this work is assuming you've got a toothbrush I can borrow," he said lightly.

"We're going to brush our teeth together. But not do anything else." Her tone reflected disbelief that this particular program had a prayer of working.

"Hey, brushing teeth together's a pretty intimate thing. Next thing you know I'll be shaving in front of you and your bras will show up in my wash. That intimacy business is a real dangerous thing to control once you let it loose. But one terrifying thing at a time…"

Well, that teasing line of chitchat got her inside the house, boots pushed off, jackets hung, a few lights turned on. It wasn't that hard to get the house relocked up and those lights turned back off and get her propelled upstairs, either.

She admitted to being whipped, no joke. He admitted to being beat, no joke. She climbed the stairs to the loft ahead of him, her stocking feet making noticeably determined thud-noisy footfalls. She aimed straight for the bathroom, where she produced a new toothbrush for him from her medicine cabinet. Like they did this every day together, he promptly layered on a thin ribbon of toothpaste and then handed her the tube. She got that determined look on her face again, but when he started brushing, so did she. By the time their mouths had respectively worked up a good head of foam, she'd loosened up and started laughing.

"This *has* to be the most unromantic thing two people could possibly do together."

"Hey, we're not doing romance tonight, remember? You gonna spit in the sink first?"

"Good grief, no. In fact, I was considering whether I could stand swallowing it so you wouldn't have to see me spit."

"Nah. The thing to do is both spit at the same time—then it's too late to be embarrassed and it's done. You never have to worry about it again." He demonstrated, giving her the courage to do it too.

"You're a real pro at handling this intimacy stuff, huh, Gautier?"

"Nobody could beat me on toothpaste issues," he assured her gravely. "Pj's are a little trickier. I mean, if I'd been expecting this sleepover, I'd have brought some. Or bought some so I could have owned a pair to bring. As it is, I'll agree to keep my shorts on...if you agree to keep your shorts on."

"I agree," she said with equal gravity.

"And naturally, we'll undress in the dark. I'm a real modest guy—which I'm sure you've noticed before."

"Um, I can't say I noticed you had a single modest bone in your entire body—"

"I do, I do. I can't possibly expose my bony knees until you know me better. But I will need a light on for a minute. You've got 3,400 pounds of debris piled in the bedroom. I could kill myself trying to find a path."

"You definitely need to be able to see," she concurred.

"And then we come down to the real tricky intimate question—"

"Birth control?"

"No, no. We're not going anywhere near that country tonight, remember? Although protection happens to be in my wallet, should that question arise any time over the next ten, twelve years. That's not a problem. I was talking about *serious* intimate questions…like which side of the bed do you have to sleep on?"

"The right side."

"Whew. Skated by that one by the skin of our teeth. I'm pretty compulsive about sleeping on the left side."

Andy figured out a relatively safe trail through the minefield of her bedroom, then switched off the lights. Clothes rustled and whooshed. Then Maggie slid between the cool smooth sheets and lay there, as still as a statue. Andy climbed in, bunched the pillow, then slid between the cool smooth sheets and lay there, too.

Silence reigned.

He didn't figure he'd sleep. Not soon. Not that night at all. Possibly never again, in fact, knowing she was lying right there next to him in a pair of underpants.

Her loft stayed blacker than a cave for a long time, no moonlight seeping through on a blustery, blizzardy night like this. The wind howled like wolves, though, hissing through the edges of her skylight. The window needed caulking, he thought practically, while his mind spun pictures of her in those underpants.

Once Maggie started laughing, he knew she'd relaxed with him again. A certain type of easy, natural teasing almost always seemed to get her to untense. He figured she'd sleep if he just stayed motionless.

He didn't plan on moving. But he wasn't likely to forget, even for a second, that she was inches away from him. Close enough to touch. Close enough to inhale her warmth, the alluring feminine scent of her skin. Close enough for his mind to have a long, challenging intellectual debate over whether her underpants would be functional white cotton or a skimpy scrap of lace. She tended toward wearing practical, sturdy clothes, suited to the seriously independent and active woman she was. But her office and bedroom gave him different clues, because in both spots she sure had girl stuff all over the place. And he knew how she kissed. For the first few moments into most kisses, Maggie was a model of self-discipline, control, and restraint, but then...gangbusters.

He'd about decided her underpants *had* to be lace. But the serious intellectual exercise of deciding what kind of underwear she favored had a predictable result. He was hard as a hammer in thirty seconds flat. Maybe twenty-five. He closed his eyes, thinking he had to be stark nuts to keep going down that road.

A fingertip suddenly touched his abdomen. His eyes shot open. He thought he'd imagined that feather-light touch, but then three more fingertips walked up his ribs. "Hey," he said.

The fingertips disappeared, but Andy barely had time to register their loss. In a sudden rustle of sheets, an entire feminine body hurled itself on his chest in their place. A distinctly bare feminine body. And even in the murky darkness, he could see her eyes were wide awake and focused. On him. "Hey," he said again—sternly. "What's going on here?"

"It was cold on my side of the bed."

"Don't lie to the law. Your body's hot as a furnace. I could have sworn this wasn't part of the program. And *where* are your underpants?"

"I don't sleep in underpants. I didn't think you'd mind. And there's been a slight change in the program. I hate to break this to you, but you can't always have things your own way. And I was thinking..."

She swooped down to nuzzle a kiss on his neck. A thoughtful, soft, tongue-wet kiss. After which she made herself more comfortable by shifting her legs around him and settling down. Where her lower abdomen happened to settle down, he was already suffering from a swollen hammer condition. Her weight wasn't heavy. In fact, her weight was so exquisitely perfect that his throat damn near went drier than the Sahara at high noon. "I'm not sure it's safe for you to do any more thinking tonight."

Safe didn't seem to impress Maggie as an immediate priority, judging from the way she was making herself at home on his body. "I was thinking...that somehow you conned me out of a really terrible mood. I'm the one who blew everything earlier. Turned into a neurotic goose on you, and since I'm not in the habit of behaving like that, I felt all shook up and awkward. Then felt even more awful that you thought I'd lied to you. Only instead of blaming me, you somehow—deviously—tricked me into feeling good about myself again."

"Um, right now, Mags, you might not want to credit me with having too many nice, honorable character traits—"

"I'll credit you with anything I damn well want to, Gautier. And there's a price to pay when you do that kind of thing to a woman. Granted, I was in love with you before, but you just forced me into loving you more. And that's it. I've had it. You don't get to say no tonight, and that's the way it's gonna be." She'd managed to make her voice sound like a bullying assertive schoolmarm, but suddenly her tone turned low and throaty. "As long as that change in program is okay with you?"

His head raised up. Hers came down. Damned if he knew if he managed to kiss her first or it was the other way around. All he knew was their lips fused like nothing in heaven or hell had better try and separate them.

A pitch-black room suddenly turned light. Maybe she'd always been sunlight for him, but now there were facets of luminous light in her eyes, the heat of a burning sun where she touched, and emotion pouring off her that showered bright, blinding fire all through him.

They'd kissed before.

Teased before.

But they hadn't been naked together. Not physically naked and not emotionally naked before, not like this. He still didn't know, not really, what had freaked her out earlier. The story about her mini-amnesia didn't ring true to him. He thought that anxiety of hers stemmed from a fear of yielding, of giving up her self-reliance. Maggie may love him, but she'd always seemed more worried than happy about their building closeness—as if she just wasn't sure what loving him was going to mean.

Andy sensed their whole future depended on his showing her. If the love was right, a man and woman could both be more independent, not less. More free. Not less. And since she didn't seem to have ever discovered that before, he figured he was working with a virgin along those lines.

But it was tough to be careful with a virgin who was peeling off his underpants. Who threw off the down comforter even though there were freezing drafts everywhere in the loft. Who was doing the brazen thing so wildly and well that maybe he wasn't supposed to notice she was trembling. Not a lot. There was just a tremor in her fingertips. And that pulse in her throat was throbbing like a fragile heartbeat. And her eyes radiated such intense seriousness that she damn near took his breath.

So he took hers. With their tongues still dueling, their lips still fused, he shifted her next to him. His hands smoothed, soothed over her shoulders and breasts and silky soft abdomen. They'd both surfaced for a lungful of air when his hand slipped down and cupped her. The soft nest of downy hair curled around his fingers and her leg reflexively shot up, trying to curl him tighter to her. She gasped his name, not the sassy teasing way she said Gautier, but Andy, Andy.

She felt damp, hot, tight around his finger. Hunger coiled through him like a whip of fire, a hunger to be inside her, claiming her, but that was no good. He had the crazy feeling he'd waited for Maggie his whole life, and no way she was escaping this night before suffering some excruciatingly painful waiting, too.

He withdrew his finger, and started skimming kisses down her throat, the hollow of her shoulder, down to her milk-white breasts. He started with the right side, but he was careful. Justice had always mattered to him. He took infinite care to not play favorites, but to lavish caressing kisses and attention equally. Her breath starting coming as shallow as a shock victim's, her hands clutching for him, which only inspired him to cause her more trouble.

His cheek rubbed, nuzzling down her abdomen. When his tongue flicked in her navel, she darn near catapulted off the bed. And she did buck when his mouth dipped lower. She'd been wildly restless, now suddenly tensed on him like a wary doe. She wasn't so sure about that kind of kiss.

He was. He wrapped her legs around him and tasted, using his tongue, his teeth, but his kisses were infinitely tender, infinitely aware that Maggie violently hated being vulnerable. A woman could make love and stay separate. A woman could make love and get off no sweat if the hormones were cooking right, but that wasn't the same as yielding. There was a kind of yielding that required trust from the gut and soul level.

That wasn't what he wanted to take from her. It's what he wanted to give her. The earthy, intimate taste of her inspired him to uncover more secrets, and suddenly she was there, her soft bare thighs clamping around his head and her back arching. She touched fire and the singe left her gasping and reaching urgently for him.

He kissed his way back up her body—a faster trip this time—then slapped the bedside table for his wallet and hurled a pillow on the floor to get rid of it. He unraveled the condom and layered kisses on her at the same time, while she was clutching at his hair, framing his face, trying to twist him around and inside her.

He drove in, thankful how ready she was for him because any patience he might have begged, borrowed or stolen was long gone. He plunged deep, filling her, claiming her, the blood rushing messages to his head that the claiming went two ways. He'd always understood Maggie's fear of yielding, her wariness of giving up her autonomy because he felt the same way. He'd never loved easily. Never loved anyone the way he felt about her. She was the someone else on the other side of the dark abyss, the one he'd never thought he'd find, the one he'd never really believed would ever be there for him.

Sex could inspire plenty of powerful emotions, but not this one. She was the one provoking all this trouble. The sensations tearing through her were tearing through him. The urgency and hunger and manic driving rhythm came from the corner of soul she owned. And when she hissed his name, convulsing around him, he came with her as if they'd both fallen in the same skyful of fireworks.

Moments later, he collapsed, drawing her with him in a cradling hold. His pulse didn't want to stop racing, his heart still thundering how perfect she was. Perfect for him, perfect with him. He stroked her until her breathing quieted, then murmured, "Maggie?"

"Andy, don't count on me having the energy for conversation for another forty-eight hours."

He kissed a smile on her brow. "Did I tell you how much I love you?"

Her head raised. Even in the fuzzy shadows he caught her grin—a sated grin, arrogant as a female cat who'd stolen a dairy full of cream and gotten away with it. "Maybe not with words at the precise moment. But believe me, you did."

Eleven

Maggie was being chased by a leather jacket. How or why the jacket represented such a menacing threat, she didn't know—even in the dream—but it was stalking her through a maze of inner-city back alleys that smelled of danger and panic. She kept turning corners, running, running, desperately trying to elude the threatening jacket, her lungs heaving so hard she couldn't think. Her dad's face showed up in a four-story-high window, saying sternly, "Maggie, I expect you to be strong," and when she stumbled around another corner, there was her mom from a second-story window, saying, "Take care of your sister." But the leather jacket was gaining, barely a heartbeat behind her. It could catch her if she let up for even a second. A trash can crashed, and she had to run past garbage, and she'd never been this lost, ever. With the pain in her side screaming, she raced around another corner, running full tilt...except that too late she realized this was a blind alley. No way out. Desperately she whirled around, and there was the jacket, its claw-like arms reaching for her throat…

Maggie's eyes popped open.

Her heart was still pumping an overload of adrenaline. But there was certainly no jacket, no family members hanging out of windows, no inner-city back alleys. Nothing but a soft pre-dawn haze shimmering shadows in her familiar bedroom. The only unusual factor anywhere in sight or sound was the man sleeping next to her.

Suddenly her heart was thudding in an entirely different way.

Maybe that thirty-second nightmare had scared her good, but it was nothing compared to the scares she'd endured through a long, long night. Andy's pager and wallet were still cluttering her nightstand. His wallet was gaping open. Maggie wasn't sure how many condoms he'd brought, but for damn sure, there wasn't a single one left in there now.

Gautier was a dangerously creative man. From the first, she'd sensed he could be trouble—but never that he'd be like tangling with an avalanche. She was tender in places she'd never been tender, whisker-burned where she'd never considered a nice, respectable good woman could possibly be whisker-burned. She turned her head, studying him.

The blackguard was lying on his stomach, sleeping as deeply as if he were in a coma—no surprise. Covers had slipped down to his waist, his hair was rumpled and disheveled, and the brackets around his eyes and mouth had eased in sleep…but they were there. The damn man's stoic character and integrity showed up even when he was dead to the world. In the middle of the night, she remembered his snuggling covers around her neck. She remembered his nuzzling her cheek against his shoulder and wrapping her in those warm, protective arms. She remembered his "I love you." She remembered his lips whispering a kiss on her temples, long past the time she could have sworn he'd dropped off himself.

The man had no conscience whatsoever about making a woman love him. And he certainly couldn't define an inhibition if it were printed in big, block letters on a road sign.

"Uh-oh."

She didn't realize he was stirring awake, until she lifted her gaze from that distinctive male mouth to his eyes. "What's that uh-oh for?"

"I saw that smile. Don't even think about it, Killer. This innocent young country boy just can't take any more—at least until I wake up."

"Innocent?"

"Well...maybe I can't claim that particular personality characteristic after last night. I just knew you'd be an incredible corrupting influence, but I sure didn't guess ahead how insatiable you'd be."

"You're calling *me* insatiable?"

Shaggy eyebrows raised in surprise. "Well, hell. It wasn't my idea to make love. You made me. You remember that part? Your insisting?"

"I remember every single detail about last night," she assured him dryly.

"So do I. I read about some of that stuff in books, but I didn't know you could really *do* them. We might have to try a couple of those things again. Practice makes perfect, they say. If I weren't so plumb worn out—"

"Gautier?"

"Yes, darlin'?"

"You just dragged me over your chest. And are using

your hands in an extremely indecent way. And I can feel certain tell-tale evidence that you're not as plumb worn out as you're claiming. Do you *always* wake up this full of blarney?''

"Do you always wake up looking this damn beautiful?" As if driven to immediately answer that question, he pulled the down comforter over their heads and kissed her. Slowly. Thoroughly. Completely.

The blasted man seemed intent on arousing memories of all the murder and mayhem he'd caused the night before, because Maggie tasted the same rattling fears all over again...that she'd never known love before him, that nothing in her life would ever be the same without Andy, that somehow he'd claimed a corner of her heart that belonged solely to him.

Those petrifying sensations were only made worse because she was kissing him back as ardently and wildly as he was kissing her. Eventually, though, they had to breathe. By the time Andy pushed back their cocoon of a comforter, the sun was peeking through the snow-covered skylight in a pink glaze. Her pulse was revved up like a jet anticipating takeoff, but he didn't seem to have that problem. He settled next to her, studying her face as if fascinated by her.

"You know, you raised an interesting question," he murmured.

"Huh? What question?" Temporarily she didn't remember any of their previous conversation. She was having trouble remembering her own name.

"The question about whether I always wake up full of blarney—and you always wake up so beautiful. It occurs to me that we could find out answers to all kinds of interesting questions like that—if my boots were parked more regularly under your bed."

Andy's voice was low and lazy as if the comment were just idle lover talk. Maggie took one look at those shrewd eyes and decided she'd better wake up. Quick. "I wasn't planning on anyone's boots being parked under my bed but yours, Gautier. But somehow I think you may have meant something a little more complicated than that. If by any chance you were suggesting our living together—"

"Maggie." His voice was chiding, his shaggy eyebrows arched in an innocent expression of surprise. "You think I'd bring up heavy waters like that before we'd even had coffee?"

She did. His palm rested on her rib cage, the heel just accidentally pressed against the swell of her breast. But before she could mention that he was an unprincipled rogue without a conscience in sight, he continued.

"It's too cold to get up yet. And too early. But while we're still snuggled up and being lazy seems a good time to daydream about some far-fetched questions. For the fun of it, no other reason. Like…have you ever thought about kids?"

"You mean those things that cry all night and go through diapers and completely destroy any chance of their parents having a sex life?"

"Uh-huh." His eyes flashed humor.

"Well…yeah. I've thought about kids. I'm crazy about 'em. I've also had some experience spoiling my nephews rotten, so I'm pretty sure I'm capable of ruining a kid or two. Sometime. You happen to have an opinion on kids?"

"You mean those things that can't talk and can't walk and cost the moon and drive their daddies into ulcers worrying about them?"

"Uh-huh." This time her eyes sparkled.

"Well…yeah. I'd like a couple of those, too. Sometime. Did you notice these were pretty easy questions so far?''

''Are you trying to warn me there are tougher ones coming?'' she asked suspiciously.

''No, no. Heavens, no.'' He hesitated. ''But I was kind of thinking about houses. You've got a fantastic place, but it's really small. And I've got a pretty good house, but there's really no ideal room for the kind of office you need.''

''Andy, do you expect me to follow this conversation when your hand is…where your hand is?''

''You want me to remove my hand?''

''I didn't say that,'' she informed him irritably.

''Well, back to houses then. The wild thought occurred to me that maybe building a place might be a solution to that down the pike. You could do the designing. We could both get our mitts wet with the actual construction. And I'd do the roof—only because you'd have me taking cyanide if I see you on another roof. But I'm thinking mountains. Trees. Privacy. Maybe a horse barn out back. Spare bedrooms, just in case. And enough closets to have ample room for his and hers, because you sure are messy, ma'am.''

Well, he'd managed to distract her. In more ways than one. ''You think we'd fight? Because I'm messy and you're not?''

''Nope. But I think we'll fight about money, because all couples do. But we already waded into money waters when you bought your car. And we already dealt with the tricky, intimate toothpaste questions. The way I see it, we've actually got some of the really terrifying stuff out of the way.''

He'd quit playing. So had she. His cheek was sharing her giant, oversized pillow, just enough distance away so

there was no missing the honesty in his eyes, the seriousness in his expression. "This is a pretty small town, Andy.
I don't think it'd go over too well for a man of the law
to just be living with a woman."

"Because it's a small town, people tend to be accept-
ing. Nor have I ever wasted a night's sleep worrying about
what other people think. But just for the record, I had
something far stickier and more binding than just living
with you in mind. But not today."

"No?" She didn't realize she was holding her breath.

"Nope." He had yet to quit watching her eyes, and
again his voice was lazy and low. "Can't see it. Bringing
up some dad-blamed honorable subject like rings when I
haven't had near my fill of your corrupting me yet. But I
did wonder if you might be free Tuesday morning.
There's some land out by Wolf Creek. Nothing developed,
but there's some good-looking sites and the land's cheap.
I can't steal more than a couple hours that morning,
but—"

She was still reeling from his mention of rings. It took
a second before she realized he'd phrased an invitation in
there. "Aw, Andy, I can't."

"Okay."

She saw the sudden shuttering of emotion in his eyes,
and instinctively reached up to touch his cheek. "Normally my work schedule's so flexible that I can easily
take off for a couple hours. But I have to drive to Boulder
on Monday afternoon, won't be back until late Tuesday.
I can't change that—because I only go into Mytron every
few weeks, other people have to schedule their time based
on when they're expecting me. I wouldn't be saying no
otherwise, Andy. If you can catch some time later in the
week, that'd be fine."

"You're sure that'd be fine?" He hooked her wrist with a velvet-careful hand.

"I'm positive."

"You're not pulling a scared thing on me, are you, Killer? Because I'm pushing you too fast?"

"You've been pushing me too fast from the day I met you, Gautier. But your being such a bully somehow hasn't stopped me from falling in love with you."

"No?"

"No." His slow grin could have made an iceberg melt. She was just thinking about demanding that he make her some coffee, but that blasted grin of his just forced her to kiss him. And that one kiss seemed to lead into another, and then another.

Andy so rarely revealed vulnerability. When she said no to his outing, she immediately realized he'd taken that as a rejection, was even braced for it. Her need to reassure him fueled a fire of emotion in Maggie. Through touch, through passion, she sought to express all he'd come to mean to her.

For the briefest moment echoes of her earlier nightmare popped into her mind, but she mentally banished those uneasy thoughts. She was still afraid of that guilt, still afraid Andy was seeing her with a lover's perfect eyes, still wary that their relationship had not been tested on anything seriously crunchy. But whether those fears were real or imagined, right now she simply had more critical priorities to attend to.

Sometimes even a big, tough, strong man needed rescuing. Sometimes a woman did, too. Andy had emotionally wrung her out the night before. The way Maggie saw it, it was her turn. And in the back of her heart, she thought, surely if they continued to build trust this way, they could conquer any problem that came their way.

* * *

At noon on Monday, Maggie had hustled into a suit and heels, had her briefcase in hand and was just slinging her overnight bag over a shoulder when the phone rang. It was her sister, and Joanna sounded frantic. The boys were in school, but the power had gone off on one side of her house. She wasn't sure if a line was down or what.

Maggie was already running late, but obviously her sister was more important than any darn job. The problem proved to be nothing more complicated than a dead fuse. Except for getting her business clothes all dusty in Joanna's basement, fixing the fuse was a piece of cake. Calming her sister down took considerably more time.

She got a late start driving into Boulder, hit mountains of traffic, and her first meetings at Mytron ran over past nine that night. By the time she checked into a motel, she crawled into bed and zonked out like a zombie. The next day started at 5 a.m. and kept up that same race-for-hell hustling pace. Still, she'd completed all her meetings by noon, and normally would have been free to drive straight home after that.

Instead she zoomed into downtown Boulder for a one o'clock appointment with Dr. Llewellyn. Boulder was decked out for Christmas no different than home, with shoppers clogging up traffic and pirating all the parking spaces. The closest spot she found was three blocks from the doc's office. By the time she'd sprinted the distance, she was almost late. And by the time she'd stripped down, put on one of those mortifying paper gowns, and was left in the examining room to wait, she felt like it was the first two seconds she'd had to catch her breath since leaving Andy.

Andy had been on her mind, though, and Andy was the sole reason she'd made the doctor's appointment.

Maggie wanted a mortifyingly thorough physical the

way she wanted an IRS audit. But she'd tried giving herself a kick in the rump to make the nightmares and anxiety attacks disappear, and that hadn't worked. She'd almost blown her relationship with Andy because one of those stupid anxiety attacks had gotten the better of her.

Enough was enough. She'd always been so strong that her inability to control that distressing, overwhelming feeling of guilt badly shamed her. But once she could see Andy was affected by her problem, shame was an inadequate reason for not taking action. For starters, she just wanted to be sure nothing medical was wrong with her.

Dr. Llewellyn strode in, white-haired and stern-eyed, his manner all business. Thankfully, her kind of doc. She didn't want to be pampered and soothed; she wanted a straight shooter. And though she hated every moment of being checked out stem to stern, she sure couldn't complain that the doc left even a toenail unexamined.

Dr. Llewellyn perched on a gray stool when he was finished. "Looks to me like you're fit as a fiddle. I wouldn't worry any more about any aftereffects from that concussion. You're doing fine," he announced.

"I already knew I was healthy as a horse," she said impatiently. "It's being nuts I was worried about."

His scrawny white eyebrows arched. "Having only spent an hour with you, I can't give you a written guarantee. But offhand, you seem remarkably sane to me, Maggie."

He was being too nice. She struggled to explain. "I told you that I had a car accident the night after Thanksgiving. When I woke up in the hospital, I couldn't remember anything about the twenty-four hours before. The doc in the emergency room told me that a little memory loss or feeling of disorientation wasn't uncommon. No reason to call it anything as highfalutin' as amnesia. If you have something traumatic happen like an accident, the mind just blocks it sometimes.''

"Right," the doctor agreed.

"Only I wasn't responsible for the accident. That's for sure. It was a drunk driver, and there were witnesses. There was absolutely no question about this.''

"Okay."

"Only…" she lifted her hands in a helpless gesture. "Only I've had nightmares ever since then. Anxiety attacks. As if I did something I should feel terribly guilty about. Except that there's nothing that I know of, and that's the only twenty-four-hour period in my whole darn life where I can't be sure what I might have done.''

Dr. Llewellyn studied her face. "Has it occurred to you that your trying to remember so hard could actually be causing this anxiety?''

"Well, yeah. But you don't understand. I'm a lot more kin to a thorn than a rose, so to speak. I can't think of a time in my life when I've run away from a problem. Maybe some sweet, fragile type of person would need to block some traumatic memory, but I'm a meaner type—''

"A mean old thorn, huh?"

"Don't laugh."

"I'm not laughing, Maggie. I can see this is hard for you to talk about, and also that it's troubling you. But there's no pill I can give you to make the memory come back. The mind just isn't like that. But I'll make a suggestion—''

"What?"

"Make a deal with yourself," the doctor suggested. "You're worried that something happened in that twenty-four hours that's causing these nightmares. Fine. Go back, talk with whoever you were with, retrace whatever you did, try and reconstruct whatever happened that day.

Maybe that'll trigger the memory, maybe it won't. But do it—give it a lion's try—and then agree with yourself to call it quits if you get nowhere. Quit beating yourself up, and accept that you've done everything you can and let it go.''

She thought about the doctor's advice on the drive home, and halfway back to White Branch, she dialed her sister on the cell phone. "I know you'll probably be right in the middle of making dinner, but I can't get home before five, and I really want to talk to you. You mind if I stop by for a few minutes?"

"Of course I don't mind, you doofus. I can't even remember the last time you asked me for anything. It's always the other way around. What's the problem, Maggie?"

She didn't want to pursue it on the phone, and she was at her sister's house in minutes. Joanna hurled the door open before Maggie'd even braked in the drive. A glass of wine was sitting on the kitchen counter waiting for her. Joanna took her coat and clucked over her as if she had two broken arms and couldn't lift a finger on her own. It took a while before Maggie could get to the problem. Joanna—of the shaky nerves and grief-haunted eyes and ditsy-dreamer ways—seemed to have transformed into a bossy monster out of nowhere.

"You never asked for my help before, sis. It's bothered me for so long. My always being the helpless one. You always being the strong one for me."

"Joanna! You're not helpless! You've just been through a terribly hard time—"

"Yeah. And I've been wallowing in it. Self-pity. The poor-me's. But you've always rescued me, Mags, even when we were little kids, even though I was the older one. And I'm not as strong as you, never will be.

But…it's awfully easy to get used to being taken care of, sis. And easy to start thinking that maybe you're as weak and helpless as people treat you. You want some more wine?''

Maggie'd barely had a sip from the first glass. Maybe she'd come to talk about her own problem, but this mattered far more. Andy had tactfully tried to suggest that she might be feeding her sister's helplessness, but it was easy to dismiss what he said as applying to someone else, not her, never her. The last thing she'd ever intended was to add to her sister's problems with confidence, yet Joanna's gently confronting her seemed to indicate she was guilty of exactly that. "I wanted you to know that you could count on me. Always. That I'd be there for you, no matter. But God, Joanna, I never meant to make you feel helpless—"

"I know you didn't. Dammit, Mags, you have a heart as big as the sky. But I could tell what you were thinking. You were afraid I'd break, weren't you, afraid I'd have a nervous breakdown?" Joanna flipped a casserole in the oven, washed her hands and turned while she was still fretfully drying them on a kitchen towel. "Well, you know what?"

"What?"

"I think I could have. Talked myself into having a nervous breakdown. I can't think of a single decision I've made in months without consulting you first. You fixed the fuses. The leaky faucets. You talked to the boys when they were having troubles. You balanced my checkbook, for Pete's sake. Even the morning I got drunk, you were so understanding—when I was acting like a jerk with no judgment. If you noticed, I poured you a glass of wine but not me. I'm not about to do that again, but the point is, *why* didn't you ever kick me in the teeth, Maggie?"

"Because I love you."

"I *know* you love me. But the real reason was because you were afraid I'd break," Joanna said patiently. "And the more everybody treated me like fragile china, the more I started believing I could break that easily, too. I'm not dead sure I can rescue myself, sis. But I need a shot at trying."

"Okay. What do you want me to do?"

"The next time I ask for help, tell me 'get lost, babe. Do it yourself.'"

"Do I have to say 'babe'?"

"Well, you don't *have* to. But it's one of those quasi-affectionate sexist words that I've always hated. So I figure it'd be a good one to get my dander up."

"And you want your dander up?"

"Uh-huh. It just might tick me off into doing something for myself—and not running to you every time the wind blows from the north. And that's entirely enough of this. That's the last word we're saying about me, and I mean it. You came here with a problem. Let's hear it."

But Maggie couldn't talk for a second. It was just such a blow. That she'd only ever wanted to help her sister and somehow ended up hurting her. And Andy had tried to tell her, but apparently she'd been too blockheaded to listen.

"Maggie, is it Andy? I already figured out that you were in love with him. You never had a glow like this. And I know you think I'm not the toughest cookie in town, but if he's done something to hurt you, I swear I'll take him out—"

"No, no, it's nothing like that." Maggie suddenly picked up the glass of forgotten wine and gulped it down. Good grief. All these weeks, she'd worried about those lost memories. All these weeks, she'd feared she was guilty of doing something terrible. And she'd come here specifically to question Joanna about Thanksgiving in hopes of triggering those memories.

But she suddenly knew.

Watching Joanna fly around the kitchen, swiping counters, wiping her hands on the kitchen towel—her sister had done exactly those things, the same way, in the hours after Thanksgiving dinner. The two women had been in the kitchen coping with the dishes and leftovers. The boys had wriggled out of KP duty faster than weasels. Both claimed they had plans. Roger was going next door to play computer games with a pal. And Colin had been going out, to places unknown.

Maggie had no idea why the complete memory came back, but it was suddenly all there. When the dishes were done, Joanna had disappeared into the bathroom. Maggie'd taken that moment to track Colin down. He'd given his mom lip about not being willing to say where he was going, and she'd intended to read him the riot act. If she'd waited two more minutes, she'd have missed him, because Colin was already outside...and that's where she found him, on the back porch, just pushing his arms into the sleeves of a leather jacket.

A good-looking, expensive leather jacket. Maggie knew perfectly well that her sister didn't have the money to buy such a garment—nor did Colin—even if the guilt and defiance in her nephew's eyes hadn't told her the whole truth.

He'd stolen it.

"Maggie," Joanna prompted her impatiently. "I don't care what the problem is. You can tell me, I swear. Give me a chance to be there for you, okay? It doesn't matter what it is. It'll be all right."

But Maggie looked at her sister, and thought, no, it's

not going to be all right. Because what her young nephew had done was bad enough. But what she'd done—to rescue Colin, to protect her sister, to just try and fix everything so the whole problem would go away—was far worse.

Right and wrong had always been black and white for Maggie. You were either an ethical person or you weren't. You didn't pick up someone else's quarter from the street. You didn't lie to save yourself from trouble. And if you were determined to do something gut-wrong, something completely against your whole code of ethics—you'd never do it in front of a child.

But she had.

She not only remembered everything about that Thanksgiving night with crystal clarity...but exactly what she'd done after that, as well.

Twelve

Andy pulled in Maggie's driveway around seven…and promptly felt his ebullient mood deflate. No tracks marred the fresh skim of new snow. No lights showed in her windows, and her car was still gone.

He had no reason to count on her being back from Boulder at this specific hour. Maggie had explained that she could never pin down timing that tightly. Because her in-office visits at Mytron were so infrequent, she stayed however long it took to get the job done.

Andy dragged a hand through his hair. He understood. He'd just really hoped she'd be home by now.

There happened to be a ring burning a hole in his pocket, picked up from the jeweler's that morning. His plan was to spring it on her Christmas Eve—not tonight. But he just wanted to be with her. It hadn't even been forty-eight hours since she'd gone on this business junket, but it seemed like a hundred years.

Making love with her had been beyond perfect. It also changed their relationship, irrevocably. Maybe that wasn't true for every couple, but Andy'd known it would be for Maggie, for him, for them. He feared she'd freak out when he brought up babies and living together and a future, but hope had snared him like a lasso when she hadn't. Possibly Mags still wasn't dead positive what marriage might mean to her independence—and he wasn't kidding himself how serious that was to her. But she loved him. He felt that love. And she couldn't doubt his loving her. They could work out anything as long as their hearts were in the same place.

Unfortunately, her body seemed to be temporarily absent from *this* place. Nothing for it but to go home and try calling her later. A guy couldn't die from being absent from his girl for forty-eight hours, could he? Suffer, yes. Die, no.

He shoved the gearshift in reverse and turned his head—just in time to see headlights flashing in his eyes. Maggie's white car zoomed into the drive next to his. He had a huge smile waiting before she'd even opened the door. Hell, he had more than that waiting for her, if she wasn't too beat from the work day and the long drive.

He saw the long legs climbing out, and greeted her with a wolf whistle. He happened to think the way her fanny filled out a pair of jeans was delectable, but he'd had no reason to catch her dressed up before. The cherry wool coat concealed her clothes, but he could see the stockings and heels just fine. Her hair was swirled up, the color of liquid honey in the moonlight.

"Is there another woman around here? Who you whistlin' at, Gautier?"

"Like I'd notice another woman with you in the universe."

"Whew. You find some charm on sale somewhere? Or was that Irish blarney you bought at a discount?"

"Couldn't be Irish blarney. I'm not Irish." He couldn't wait any longer to descend on her for a kiss. While she was juggling a briefcase and tote and purse and had her hands completely full seemed an ideal moment to take advantage. He nudged her chin up, saw that soft red mouth and promptly swooped down for a taste.

It took him a second to realize that her lips were trembling under his. Even when he realized, he first took that trembling as responsiveness...when Maggie was in the mood, she'd never been stingy about letting him know it. But a few seconds later, his mind registered that her shoulders were rigidly stiff with tension.

He lifted his head, confused by what was happening. No matter how bright the moonlight, the illumination just wasn't clear enough to really study her. Her face seemed milky pale, though. And her eyes...she wasn't crying? But he'd never seen anything get Maggie down; she charged up anywhere near a problem and grabbed for the challenge with both hands. And her eyes looked so luminous with emotion that Andy just couldn't guess what was going on with her. "Something's wrong? You didn't rob any banks in Boulder, did you, Killer?"

He thought she'd smile at the joke. Instead she seemed to turn even paler, and though she started to answer, no words seemed to come out.

"Hey." He touched her cheek, concerned now. "Did something happen? Some problem come up with your work?"

She found her voice. "No, work went fine. Really fine, in fact. My guys were great, got a ton done..."

"See an accident on the freeway? Run into some rough traffic?"

"No. Nothing like that. But Andy..."

When she hesitated, he moved—grabbed her gear all up in one hand and cuddled an arm around her shoulder with the other. "Let's go inside, okay? Get your shoes and coat off, get you set down."

She went in, but there was sure no getting her set down. She didn't want an alcoholic drink, but he talked her into some tea. He made the tea, but then she didn't drink that either. And she pushed off her shoes and shed the wool coat, revealing a warm, snuggly sweaterdress in a forest green that perfectly matched her eyes. But she hugged her arms under her chest like she was cold, and nothing could make her sit down.

"I have to tell you something, Andy."

"So shoot. For God's sake, you know you can tell me anything—"

"Well, maybe not this. In fact, I considered not telling you. But we've always been honest with each other. And honesty's too important to both of us, because we've been burned in other relationships when other people tried hiding their real feelings about things—"

"Mags, that's old ground. You know I feel exactly the same way, so just cut to the chase." He leaned back against the kitchen counter, giving her space to get the pacing out of her system.

"I know you never believed my little amnesia problem was a big deal."

This was what that sick-dread anxiety in her eyes was all about? "I believed it was troubling for you."

"Well, I remembered. Everything that happened in those twenty-four hours before my car accident."

"So, that's great—"

"Not exactly." She reached up to yank the pins out of her hair. The smooth chignon tumbled loose, becoming more disheveled when she dragged her hands through it. She clipped out this whole story about finding Colin wearing a stolen jacket as he was leaving the house after Thanksgiving dinner. She knew it was stolen—knew it because her nephew couldn't possibly afford such a jacket and neither could her sister. And Colin didn't try to lie once she confronted him.

Andy felt his lawman's pulse start thumping when she relayed the business about the theft. Impossible not to feel the adrenaline push; it was his whole nature to take charge with that kind of problem. But he tried to tamp down that instinct until he got the whole story clear. "Okay. So your nephew stole that jacket. And you love him, so that whole problem naturally upset you. But now you know for positive—there was no reason for you to have those guilty dreams. You didn't do anything yourself—"

"But I did, Andy." She pivoted around, swallowed hard, faced his eyes. "This just isn't easy to explain. Colin—I know he did a bad thing, but I swear he's got a good heart clear through. I told you he got in some trouble last year, running with a hotshot group of kids that had a lot of money, thinking he'd be accepted if he kept up with them? But that was about his dad dying. Grief coming out in the form of anger, and I think part of his acting out was his trying to get his mom's attention, too. For a while there it had to feel like he lost both parents, because Joanna was so caught up in her own grief—"

"Let's get past the psychology. What'd *you* do?"

She stiffened at his clipped tone. "I'm trying to tell you. I was shook up when I found him with the jacket. And all I could think about was…fixing this. Rescuing Colin, so he wouldn't get in trouble. And my sis, especially on that holiday, just seemed so brittle and emotionally shaky. I was afraid a serious problem could be the straw that broke the camel's back. All I could think about was doing whatever I had to do to make it go away—''

"Somehow I'm getting more nervous the more you're talking. What the hell did you *do?*''

Her eyes shot to the ceiling. "I took the jacket from Colin. Went home. The next afternoon—you know how crowded the stores are the day after Thanksgiving?—I wore the jacket under my regular coat. Went into Mulliker's. Made out like I was shopping for men's jackets. There were all these people around...and those expensive coats all have this theft prevention chain thing. So I had to fool the salesman into unlocking the chain. And then I had to wait and wait until no one was looking—and I put the jacket back.''

Andy'd listened. But he just couldn't believe. "Let me get this straight. The kid stole the jacket, but you let him off the hook altogether. No penalty, no punishment, nothing about his taking responsibility for what he did.''

"Well, hindsight's cheap, but I realize now Colin was asking for me to do something. After the accident, he turned into this hovering, helpful angel. Too much so. If I'd just remembered what had happened, maybe I'd have...'' Her voice trailed off as she looked at his face. "No point in further explaining, is there? You said it right.''

"And you didn't tell your sis. Even though this was *her* kid, her problem, and just maybe it wasn't even your business to interfere.''

"You're right on that, too,'' she said quietly.

"Didn't we talk before about your overprotecting your sister? You never even gave her a chance to step up to the plate, even though that's sure as hell a problem I'd think she has a right to know regarding her own son.''

"You're right again.''

"And then you go in the store, like a thief yourself—as if un-stealing this jacket can make everything all right. You realize you could have been arrested yourself? Dammit, where was your *head?*"

Maggie took a long breath, looking at him, then away. Something changed in her eyes. She'd been so anxious, but now she went real still. "My head was in Poughkeepsie. I made a mistake. A bad one. But all along, I've been scared of exactly this with you—"

"Scared of what?"

"Scared that you were always so sure I'd never do anything really wrong. Scared when you said you loved me—that you never meant it." She shook her head, swiftly, fiercely. "This isn't going to work. I think it'd be best if you go."

"Go?" He felt a stabbing sensation in his chest, but she was making no sense. How she'd leapt from her nephew's theft to his loving her confused him completely.

But she didn't look confused. She just looked...beaten. "The whole relationship came so easily to us. Too easily. I just kept having the feeling that you were counting on me...to be someone I wasn't. Could never be. You want it in spades? I make huge mistakes, Gautier. If you thought I'd never hurt you, never screw up in serious ways...I was always doomed to let you down sometime. I'm not that 'good woman' you think I am. I never was."

Andy wasn't quite sure how he ended up on the winter-cold side of her back door, but he seemed to have been kicked out.

Unbelievable. Mags was furious with *him? He* wasn't the one who'd done anything wrong.

He stomped to his car, slapped the gearshift in reverse and barrelled out of her drive. Instead of heading home, he aimed for the sheriff's office. It was the one place he was likely guaranteed dead silence. His deputies were on call that night, but they weren't likely to budge from their home fires unless there was trouble. On a night this close to Christmas, the office was sure to be as deserted and quiet as a morgue.

He slumped in his office chair, dug the ring box out of his pocket, and popped it open on the desk...then stared at it good and hard.

He'd considered letting Maggie pick it out herself. With her fierce independent streak, she'd probably want to choose what she wanted, get practical about it. But that was precisely why he'd picked it out on his own. She'd be practical. He just knew it. He also figured she'd argue about being the plain gold band type, so he'd gotten her the plain gold band. He'd just added a marquise diamond to go with it, with emeralds flanking the diamond—green, like the woods in sunlight. Which she loved. And like her eyes. Which he loved.

Well, that was all blown. Damn woman had thrown him out of her life. Because *she'd* made a mistake.

Andy bolted out of his chair, stalked the circumference of the office, then threw himself in the chair again. Everyone had moments of insanity. Men. Women. Maggie. Certainly he'd encountered Maggie's brand of goofiness before this. She was damn near a zealot on owing nobody—like buying a car with cash. And she was a lioness about protecting her family and her sister—way, way overprotective. And climbing on the roof to handle a leak herself in the middle of winter—that was past goofy and just plain blockheaded.

So she had some flaws. They happened to be flaws he loved right along with the rest of her.

He launched out of his chair again, paced another circle

around the office, then hurled himself back in the chair and stared at the damned ring again. Craziest thing he'd ever heard—her being mad when he hadn't done a thing; she was the one who'd made the mistake.

But that sick, sad look in her eyes kept haunting his mind. And he started to think about all the joking he'd done, teasing her about the seven deadly sins, her robbing banks, calling her Killer. Maybe she *had* gotten the idea he expected her to be perfect. Not about cars and roofs and sisters. But down deep. At the level where everybody hid their secrets.

He thought about the way she'd blocked that memory for all these weeks—hell, he could hardly think of a soul who'd lose a night's sleep over such a problem. But Maggie was different. Something like that was always going to eat her alive. She never compromised on ethics. She took them as gut seriously as he did.

And he'd yelled at her.

Judged her.

Andy stared out the window, watching the snowflakes drift down, dancing under the Christmas lights on Main Street...but it wasn't the magic of snowflakes he saw. Maggie expected herself to solve every problem; she leaned on nobody—including him. Damn woman was probably strong enough to run a small country without a lick of help, but that huge heart of hers was her Achilles' heel. He'd seen it every time she talked about her sister. When it came to family, she gave love generously, blindly, past right or wrong, and no matter what the risk to herself.

And she'd given the same kind of love to him. Taking him into her heart and life, even though he'd rushed her, even though he threatened that loss of independence she was so wary of risking. All along, she hadn't really counted on him to support her. To come through. To stand by her.

And when something finally happened to test what his love really meant, he'd yelled at her.

Failed her.

She could do this, Maggie told herself. A peanut butter sandwich had long since dried out on the kitchen counter, uneaten. Upstairs, the business clothes she'd peeled off were still heaped on the floor, and the long, comforting soak in the tub she'd intended hadn't lasted five minutes.

Now, snuggled in her old green robe, she stared at her computer screen. She'd brought home a full briefcase of new work from Boulder. There was nothing she immediately had or wanted to do, but that wasn't the point. Getting through the next few hours was the point. And if she could just make herself concentrate for a few hours, then maybe she could find another way to get through the hours after that.

Only her fingers refused to stay on the keyboard keys. Her hands kept reaching up, rubbing her face, covering her eyes. Her whole body ached like flu. Her eyes burned. Her heart felt like it was being choked tight by a wrestler's fist.

She'd made such a mess of everything. Andy. Her sister. Colin. But she knew what to do about the family problems,—come clean, make amends, quit rescuing her sister. Before leaving Joanna's house, she'd started that process by confessing the whole jacket episode to Joanna and bringing Colin into the act as well. Colin had honestly seemed relieved to have his guilt out in the open, and her sis had been forgiving, but Maggie knew it wasn't going to be that easy. Real change took work. She needed to seriously work at breaking her patterns of behavior, but at least she had answers. She knew what had to be done to make things right.

Andy was different, because she had no answers on how to make anything right with him. Her heart felt sliced in two. The missing half irrevocably belonged to Andy, only she'd let him down—the one damn man in the whole universe that she'd never wanted to disappoint. His condemnation had cut her sharper than a razor, and no, of course she'd never expected him to be thrilled at her part in the theft story. But silence hadn't been a choice either. He'd known about her amnesia problem, so pretending she'd never recovered her memory would never have worked. More to the point, it would have been lying, and Maggie had had that done to her in relationships before. She'd thought Andy was the one person on earth she could be gut-honest with. And they had nothing worth saving if they couldn't trust each other with honesty the same way.

When she heard the brring of the back doorbell, she tensed, dropping her hands.

The bell rang again. Still she didn't move. It was almost ten, late for any normal visitor, so she didn't need any psychic skill to guess it had to be Andy. Her whole life she'd prided herself on strength, but right now her eyes were burning and her stomach was churning and she felt shakier than a wilted dandelion. She needed time. She had to have some time. She just couldn't take being hurt any more, not right now, not tonight.

A hand lay relentlessly flat on the doorbell. And didn't let up.

Since her car was in the drive, the visitor had to realize she was choosing not to answer the door. Still, he seemed prepared to lie on that doorbell all night. She swallowed, pushed herself out of the chair and padded barefoot through the kitchen to the back hall. Every muscle in her body braced as she opened the door.

The doorbell immediately quit screeching. And she'd half expected to see the shaggy dark hair, the shoulders filling out an alpaca jacket. But blocking her view of his face completely was a tree.

"Just move aside and let me get this in, Killer. It's heavier than lead—"

"Andy, I—"

"Yeah, I know. You don't want to talk to me, don't want to see me. But just let me put this down in your living room, okay? It's not cut—it's still in a root ball in a pot, so you can plant it later. But that's what's making it so heavy. And as soon as I put it down, I'll leave right away."

Without waiting for her acquiescence, he charged right past her. The Norfolk pine brushed past her face, the scent as fresh as Christmas. The tree was a beauty of an adolescent, just under four feet, and already decorated with strands of lights that shifted and swayed drunkenly as Andy shot down to her living room. He almost tripped on one trailing strand.

Maggie saw no way that she could avoid helping him. He was going to kill himself if she didn't hustle to pick up the strand. And she didn't want to look at the tree— even the first glimpse had made her eyes feel blister-hot with the sudden threat of tears—but she had to move a chair or he'd have no place to set it down.

The instant she moved the chair—without another word to her—he plunked the tree down by the glass doors. Technically the job was done then. Only he didn't seem to think so. First he fussed around, finding a place to plug in the lights. Then he hiked back outside to his car, and came back in carrying a huge red blanket to wrap around the base. Somewhere in the folds of the blanket, Maggie thought she saw the glimpse of a tiny package with a silver bow—but she didn't look closer. She didn't do anything but stand with her arms folded tight, trying to stay out of his way, trying not to look like she was as rattled as a leaf in a lightning storm.

Andy stood up after fussing with the blanket, and made a frowning attempt to rearrange the drunken light strands—in a man's version of artistic. He made them worse. Not better. Which for some unknown reason made her eyes feel stinging hot all over again. His voice, unlike her nerves, was as calm and soothing as melted butter. "I had to do the tree, Mags. It just wasn't right—that you'd been part of putting a tree up at my house, and then you didn't have one. And you and I are peas in a pod that way, aren't we? Neither of us can sit still for two seconds when something's wrong."

She wanted to thank him for the tree, just get any conversation over with that had to be. But there was no getting words past the lump in her throat, not at that instant. And Andy—contrary to his reassuring claim about leaving—suddenly pushed off his jacket and tossed it on the couch.

"You're not talking to me. I understand that. I wouldn't be talking to me in your shoes either. I let you down, Killer."

She pushed the words out, because that misconception simply had to be corrected. "I'm the one who let you down."

"Nope." He wasn't crowding her, standing with a hearth between them. But he wasn't standing very far from her either. "I only wish I could think up an excuse for acting so dumb. The best I can try and explain is that you started telling me about a theft, and I got a knee-jerk instinct to respond as a lawman.''

"You *are* a lawman.''

"Not with you. There's no badge with you, Maggie. I'm just your lover—was," he swiftly corrected himself. "But I was sick after I left. Remembering how those nightmares and anxiety attacks had been bugging you. All that guilt. All that stress. You were crucifying yourself with those nightmares—and I kept trying to tease you out of taking them so seriously.''

Well, he was forcing her to talk. "Andy, there was nothing wrong with that," she said impatiently. "You didn't know, and neither did I, that I'd done something so serious.''

"Yeah, you tried to rescue your family. Offhand, I'd say anybody who ever loved could understand what you did. You're the only one thinking of it as a hanging crime.'' Andy glanced through her glass doors at the snowflakes drifting down like crystals in the moonlight. "I realized after I left, that's what you needed. Someone to help you get over it. See past it. Someone to bully you into forgiving yourself, since you seem to be too block-headed to do it on your own.''

The blockheaded insult put a new lump in her throat. He'd just said it so tenderly. "Gautier, it was no small thing I did. Not by your values. And not by mine.''

"Maybe it wasn't real wise. But so far I haven't met anybody in life who was always capable of being wise. And I have a theory—''

"A theory?''

He nodded swiftly. "A theory that if you're gonna commit any more wild, amoral, immoral crimes in the future, it'd be best if you married a lawman. I'm not say-ing that should be me, mind you—''

"No?" He'd quit looking at those snowflakes. He was looking at her now. Only at her. Like nothing else was in that room, not the Christmas tree, not the fire snapping in her hearth, nothing.

"No, no, I realize I blew my chances with you. You break trust with somebody—they'd be damn dumb to give you a second shot. But I've got a theory about the kind of guy that's right for you. You've got a thing about self-reliance, your autonomy. Any man trying to pin you down—he's no good. It has to be a man who respects independence, respects that there's some things you have to do your own way, respects that you actually need a little danger and challenge from time to time. And then there's that brave face you put on for the world. It's real, that courage and strength. But those rare times when life gets you down...you need a guy who'll be there for you. A guy who makes you feel safe, even when you're not strong. Someone you trust at the gut level, because you know, good times, bad times, all times, he'll be there."

Well, for Pete's sake. Maggie never cried, and certainly never in a crisis. That always when somebody had to stand up and be tough, because nobody else ever wanted that job. But Andy knew perfectly well that he wasn't describing some stranger. And he was looking at her like she was the sun and the moon and more precious than both.

She swiped at her cheek, lifted her chin. "Did you...have anyone in mind? About this guy for me?"

"No, no. I wouldn't presume. But I think a couple kids belong in that picture. And a place designed with both your needs in mind. And dreams are another thing. You and your guy, now, they don't have to have the same dreams. But taking a chance on the future together, that's no small thing. If you can't share your dreams together, you've got nothing.''

"Anything else?'' She only asked to give herself a minute to catch some control, but it wasn't working. She just couldn't take much more of this. She'd been so sure that she'd irrevocably let Andy down.

"Hell, yeah. The sex has to be good. Considering your amoral, immoral, wanton ways, I'd say he better be a fast learner. I don't know as an innocent old country boy could cut the mustard—unless you're willing to give him brownie points for stamina and enthusiasm. And then there's one last critical ingredient this guy has to have—''

"*What?*''

Perhaps he sensed she was exasperated with herself, not him, because Andy used the excuse to step closer. He yanked a handkerchief from his pocket, mopped her eyes, then held it securely over her nose. "Blow,'' he ordered.

"Forget it. I'm not blowing my nose in front of you!''

"Trust me, Mags, this is one of those toothpaste things—you just have to do it once and then you never have to feel embarrassed again.''

She blew like a foghorn, thinking that she *did* trust him. About those toothpaste things. About everything. She could be herself with him, no fibs, no ever having to pretend. It was part of her loving him so much, part of why her heart had felt ripped raw-open when she thought her mistake had killed what they had together.

But Andy's words had turned that pain around. Whatever mistakes she'd made…he wasn't one of them. Everything he said revealed how completely he understood what mattered to her. As she hoped she understood what he needed in his life. "So…what's this last critical ingredient this mystery guy has to have?''

"Love,'' Andy said quietly, gravely. "I never did think

love was more important than all the rest. It isn't. The whole package has to be there. Trust, respect, honor, dreaming, good sex. But if you were rating love on a scale of one to ten, I'd still give it a ninety-eight." He swallowed, and his voice turned hoarse. "And I love you more than life, Maggie."

She launched herself into his arms, thinking that the darn man had deliberately cleared her sinuses because he'd probably expected she'd do just this. Grab him. Do her utmost best to kiss him senseless, kiss him witless, kiss him until neither of them had an ounce of oxygen left.

She didn't need oxygen. She needed the warm, secure arms of her lawman. "And I love you back," she said fiercely. "Oh, Andy, I thought I'd lost you."

"I think we just found each other—in every way that matters. There's a ring under the tree—"

"And I'd love to see it. I'd love it on my finger. In just a minute," she whispered, and kissed him again with a brimming full heart.

She'd clung to independence for so long. She'd never believed she'd find anyone who could know her—down at that mistake-making flawed core—and still love her. But Andy not only did; she'd come to understand he had the same painful vulnerability. He was terrible at forgiving his own mistakes, no different than her.

She'd be there for him. He might not be dead positive of that now, but she had a lifetime to make her lawman feel infinitely, securely loved. From the corner of her eye, she saw the twinkling lights of her Christmas tree—their tree. Their magic. And she felt the fierce, sharp wondrous tug of love everywhere he touched, everywhere she kissed…more magic. Their magic. They knelt together, whispering promises for the future, both of them knowing their love was grounded in reality. The best kind of magic of all.

* * * * * *

*Bestselling author Jennifer Greene will be back
to bring you another wonderful story
coming in January. Don't miss*
THE HONOR BOUND GROOM, *the
first exciting book of Silhouette Desire's special*
**FORTUNE'S CHILDREN:
BRIDES OF FORTUNE** *continuity.*

Take 2 bestselling love stories FREE

Plus get a FREE surprise gift!

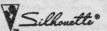

For a limited time, Harlequin and Silhouette have an offer you just can't refuse.

In November and December 1998:

BUY **ANY** TWO HARLEQUIN
OR SILHOUETTE BOOKS and
SAVE $10.00
off future purchases

OR BUY ANY THREE HARLEQUIN OR SILHOUETTE BOOKS
AND **SAVE $20.00** OFF FUTURE PURCHASES!

(each coupon is good for $1.00 off the purchase of two
Harlequin or Silhouette books)

JUST BUY 2 HARLEQUIN OR SILHOUETTE BOOKS, SEND US YOUR
NAME, ADDRESS AND 2 PROOFS OF PURCHASE (CASH REGISTER
RECEIPTS) AND HARLEQUIN WILL SEND YOU A COUPON BOOKLET
WORTH **$10.00 OFF** FUTURE PURCHASES OF HARLEQUIN OR
SILHOUETTE BOOKS IN 1999. SEND US 3 PROOFS OF PURCHASE AND
WE WILL SEND YOU 2 COUPON BOOKLETS WITH A TOTAL SAVING OF
$20.00. (ALLOW 4-6 WEEKS DELIVERY) OFFER EXPIRES
DECEMBER 31, 1998.

I accept your offer! Please send me a coupon booklet(s), to:

NAME: _____

ADDRESS: _____

CITY: _____ STATE/PROV.: _____ POSTAL/ZIP CODE: _____

Send your name and address, along with your cash register
receipts for proofs of purchase, to:

In the U.S.	**In Canada**
Harlequin Books	**Harlequin Books**
P.O. Box 9057	**P.O. Box 622**
Buffalo, NY	**Fort Erie, Ontario**
14269	**L2A 5X3**

PHQ4982

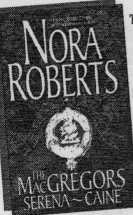

SILHOUETTE® Desire®

COMING NEXT MONTH